A Book of Monsters

A BOOK OF
MONSTERS

Ruth Manning-Sanders

ILLUSTRATED BY
ROBIN JACQUES

METHUEN CHILDREN'S BOOKS
London

First published in Great Britain 1975
by Methuen Children's Books Ltd
11 New Fetter Lane, London EC4P 4EE
Copyright © 1975 Ruth Manning-Sanders
Printed in Great Britain by Ebenezer Baylis & Son Limited
The Trinity Press, Worcester, and London

ISBN 0 416 81440 9

Contents

Foreword

There is something rather pathetic about monsters. After all, they didn't make themselves; they can't help being huge and hideous. And if they are usually fierce and cruel – well, if everyone hated and feared you, and ran screaming from the sight of you, wouldn't that be enough to give you a grudge against all humanity? It is really a wonder that any of them are kind-hearted; and yet some of them are. Take *Monster Copper Forehead*, for instance, in the Russian story: all he wants to make him feel happy is someone to love and look after. He regards human beings rather as we regard a litter of puppies – charming little creatures to be petted and cared for. And at the end of the story we find that he can even sacrifice his own happiness for the happiness of someone he loves.

Then there is the monster in *The Golden Valley*, a Sicilian story, for whom the finding of a human friend makes the whole world to shine. And *Monster Dunber*, in the story that comes from Bohemia, though he does threaten to roast the naughty girl who steals his gold chain, is not really a bad-hearted old fellow. At the end of the story we find him announcing that he won't interfere with the people in the valley as long as they don't interfere with him.

And what about that queerity, the *Great Golloping Wolf*, in another Russian story? He certainly has his good points. True, he does all but swallow down Stepan. But when he finds out – just in time – that Stepan is his sister's husband, then he goes to no end of trouble to help them both.

As for eating people (a habit among monsters), we have to remember that they look upon the eating of human beings precisely as we look upon the eating of beef and mutton.

There are also the unfortunate monsters, not really monsters at all, but men who have been turned into their horrible shape by malice or mishap. We find one of these unfortunates, in the Swedish story *Prince Lindworm*, who is born a monster owing to his mother's carelessness. And we find another in *The Singing Leaves* (a story from the Tyrol): a young emperor, whom the malice of a flouted sorceress has turned into a monster until such time as a maiden falls in love with him and consents to be his wife.

And so, having sorted out the monsters for whom we can make excuses and sympathize with, we are left with the truly brutish and horrible ones: the *Seven Monsters* in the African story, for instance, who can't even agree among themselves – each one smacking his lips over the thought of swallowing down the king's daughter; and *Monster Horisto* in the Macedonian story, with his cunning scheming to get poor little Pentalina into his cooking pot, and to feast his monster-comrades on her tender flesh. *The Monster in the Mill* (another Macedonian story) is no better, though much more stupid.

Then there is that great stupid *Gogo* in the West African story *Lu-bo-bo* who will not even pay heed to the complaints of his own stomach, but eats and eats until he bursts. And the monster in *The Story of the Three Young Shepherds* (from Transylvania) whose high opinion of himself and cruel greedy ways, though they bode ill for the young shepherds, yet in the end are brought to nothing by the resourcefulness of a little sparrow.

Lastly we come to the story told by the Tartars, the story of the terrible woman monster Ubir, whose appetite and capacity for devouring all she sets eyes on seems to outdo even the greed of other monsters. Yes, she deserves her fate; and when she is finally laid low by a silver bullet in her brain, all we can say is that the world is well rid of her.

So here you have them, in these twelve stories: some monsters we can find excuses for, and even sympathize with; and other monsters for whom no good word can be said, nor any reason found for their existence – unless it be to test the courage and ingenuity of those who bring about their downfall.

1 · *Ubir*

There was a pretty girl called Rosalie, and she had three brothers. But the brothers were all married and had gone away to homes of their own. So now Rosalie lived by herself.

Not far from Rosalie's cottage was a forest. And in the forest lived Ubir, the huge woman-monster, who was always hungry, and who prowled by day and by night seeking food, and devouring men and cattle, and anything else she could get hold of.

Now Rosalie loved her brothers, and it was a long time since she had seen them. So one evening she said to herself, 'I will harness my little horse into my little carriage and take a drive to visit my brothers. I will visit them each in turn. Tomorrow I will visit Vanka, my eldest brother, the day after tomorrow I will visit Yury, my middle brother, and on the third day I will visit Sidor, my youngest brother.'

Next morning Rosalie got up very early, before dawn, and baked some cakes to take as a present to her brother Vanka. She put the cakes neatly in a basket on the kitchen table, and then went to the stable to harness her little horse into her little carriage.

But that morning the monster Ubir was on the prowl – she had been on the prowl all night, seeking food and finding none, and she was very, very hungry. So, whilst Rosalie was in the stable, it happened that Ubir passed by the cottage and smelled the newly baked cakes.

Sniff, sniff, sniff went Ubir's long nose, and *creak, creak, creak* went Ubir's great feet, walking on tiptoe outside Rosalie's kitchen window. And softly, softly Ubir's great hand lifted the window sash, and picked up the cake basket.

Ah ha! Into Ubir's great mouth, and down into Ubir's

great stomach, went basket, cakes and all – and Ubir walked off.

So, when Rosalie, having harnessed her little horse into her little carriage, came back into the kitchen – well, there: no cakes and no basket! But Rosalie wasn't going to visit her brother, Vanka, empty-handed. Quickly she set to and baked more cakes, put them in another basket, jumped into her little carriage, and drove off. And she hadn't driven more than a mile when she heard a great voice shouting behind her, 'Little Rosalie, wait, my mouth is watering!'

Rosalie looks round. Oh, oh! There is huge monster Ubir pounding along the road!

What to do? Rosalie takes a cake from the basket and flings it behind her. Ubir stops to pick up the cake and cram it into her mouth – then on she comes again.

'Little Rosalie, wait!' roars the great voice. 'My boots are pinching me!'

Rosalie flings another cake behind her. Ubir stops to pick it up, crams it into her huge mouth, comes on again.

'Little Rosalie, wait! My ankles are aching!'

Rosalie throws down another cake. Ubir stops to pick it up, then on she comes again. Ubir's great feet are pounding, pounding, the little horse is galloping, galloping, Ubir's great voice is roaring, roaring, 'Little Rosalie, wait, wait!' Rosalie throws out another cake, Ubir stops to swallow it, comes on again. Rosalie throws out cake after cake, until there are no cakes left; the basket is empty, and still Ubir comes pounding on, 'Little Rosalie, wait, little Rosalie, wait!' Rosalie throws out the empty basket, Ubir picks it up, swallows it down, comes on again. 'Little Rosalie, wait, wait!'

Rosalie jumps from the carriage, takes off a wheel, flings it behind her, jumps back into the carriage, whips up the little horse. The little horse is galloping, galloping, the carriage is rocking along on three wheels, Ubir has picked up the fourth wheel and swallowed it, and still she comes pounding on.

'Little Rosalie, wait, my stomach is growling!'

Rosalie jumps out of the carriage, takes off another wheel, flings it behind her, jumps into the carriage again, and drives on. The little carriage is bumping along on two wheels, Ubir swallows down the third wheel, then she comes pounding on.

'Little Rosalie, wait, my stomach is not yet full!'

Rosalie pulls up, takes off another wheel, flings it behind her, drives on. Ubir stops to swallow down the wheel, comes pounding on again.

'Little Rosalie, wait! My heart is thumping against my ribs!'

Rosalie takes off the last wheel, flings it behind her, drives on. The little horse is galloping, galloping, the carriage is bouncing and dragging, Ubir has swallowed down the last wheel, and still she comes pounding on.

'Little Rosalie, wait, wait! My heart is bursting!'

Rosalie jumps out of the carriage, leaves it behind her, scrambles on to the back of the little horse, gallops away.

Ubir stops to pick up the carriage. She crams it into her great mouth, she swallows it down. She is a long time swallowing that carriage, and Rosalie now has a good start. But, oh me, let the little horse gallop fast as he will, Ubir runs faster.

Now she is catching up again. 'Little Rosalie wait, I have lost a boot, and a thorn sticks in my toe.'

The little horse is galloping, galloping, but Ubir is coming nearer and nearer, she catches the little horse by the tail, Rosalie slips off the back of the little horse and runs, runs. Ubir tosses the little horse head first into her great mouth, and swallows him down.

But the little horse kicks and bites; he makes such a commotion in Ubir's stomach that Ubir sicks him up and spits him out. The little horse turns and gallops home, and Ubir races on after Rosalie. Rosalie takes off her head scarf and flings it behind her. Ubir stops to pick it up and swallow it, then she comes pounding on. Rosalie takes off her dress and flings it behind her. Ubir stops to swallow down the dress, then she comes pounding on. Rosalie flings off her shoes, her stockings, her petticoat, her drawers, Ubir stops to pick them up and swallow them, one after the other; then she comes pounding on. . . .

Now the sun has set. Now it is twilight. Now it is night. Rosalie is still running, and Ubir is still following her.

'Little Rosalie, my little supper, wait! But where are you, my little supper? I cannot see you in the darkness!'

And in the darkness, Rosalie, having dodged down one lane and up another, comes out into the village street at her brother Vanka's door.

Knock, knock, knock!

> '*Open the door, my brother Vanka,*
> *Open the door to me,*
> *I am here in the night, my brother, my brother,*
> *Your sister Rosalie.*
>
> '*Through day and through dusk and through dark, brother,*
> *Great Ubir has chased me sore,*

Oh, open and let me in, brother,
For I can run no more!'

Vanka was in bed. When he heard the knocking he got up, lit a candle, and went cautiously downstairs. Rosalie's voice was hoarse with weariness and terror; Vanka did not recognize it. He peered through the keyhole, and saw a girl's naked feet and legs. His sister Rosalie? No, indeed!

'Go away!' he shouted. 'My sister Rosalie is a modest maiden. *She* does not come naked to knock at men's doors in the middle of the night!'

And he stamped upstairs again.

'Oh my brother, my brother!' Rosalie turned from the door and fled on. Farther down the street she came to her brother Yury's house.

Knock, knock, knock!

> 'Open the door, my brother Yury,
> Open the door to me,
> Oh, how can you bar your door, brother,
> Against poor Rosalie?
>
> 'This morning I baked some cakes, brother,
> But Ubir swallowed them down,
> She swallowed my horse and my carriage, brother,
> She swallowed my best silk gown.
>
> 'And here I stand in my nakedness, brother,
> A shame for the world to see —
> Oh, open, open your door, brother,
> Or Ubir will swallow me!'

Yury had been fast asleep when the knocking wakened him. No more than Vanka did Yury recognize Rosalie's hoarse voice. He didn't even trouble to go downstairs. He opened the window, shouted 'Go away!', slammed the window, and went back to bed.

Rosalie turned from the door. Now she could hear Ubir's great feet trampling down the street behind her. Desperately she ran on. At the very end of the street she came to her brother Sidor's house, and there desperately she knocked.

Knock, knock, knock!

> 'Open the door, my brother Sidor,
> Open, open to me,
> Through the day, through the night, my brother, my brother,
> Great Ubir has followed me.
>
> 'Hark, hark, her heavy feet,
> Stamping, stamping down the street!
> Oh, brother Sidor, rescue me,
> Your little sister, Rosalie!'

Sidor lay in bed beside his wife. 'Listen,' he said, 'some poor wench out there, begging shelter in the name of our sister, Rosalie!'

Sidor's wife opened her eyes and yawned. 'What a horrible hoarse voice! Impertinent baggage! Tell her to go away!'

'But then,' said Sidor, 'perhaps she has nowhere to go? Perhaps we should let her in?'

'No, no, she may be a thief! Send her away!' said Sidor's wife.

So Sidor put his head out of the window. He couldn't see who stood below under the porch. 'I can't let you in at this time of night, when all good women are in their beds,' he called. 'But if you have nowhere better to go, you may shelter in my barn.'

Rosalie ran to the barn. And just as she reached it, Ubir came stamping into the yard. 'Ah, my little supper, my sweet tasty little supper, I smell you, I smell you!'

In the darkness Ubir reached out her great hand and caught Rosalie by the hair. Ah no! Ah no! Rosalie screamed, wrenched herself free, left a lock of her hair in Ubir's fist, rushed into the barn, and barred the door.

'My little supper, where are you? Where have you hidden yourself?'

The ground shook under Ubir's feet as she floundered this way and that about the yard in the blackness of night. She was making such an uproar that every dog in the village began to bark: lights appeared at windows, men were starting from their beds, asking, 'What's happening? What's that roaring? What's that shaking? An earthquake surely!' 'No, boys, thunder! That's what it is!' 'But I didn't see any lightning!' 'Well it must be thunder – what else?' 'And mighty close!' 'Out with the lights, pull your bed into the middle of the room, say a prayer, and sleep if you can! Hark – there again!'

With a roar of rage that set doors and windows rattling, and the very walls of the houses shuddering, Ubir strode off into the night. . . .

In the morning, Sidor remembered the poor wench he had sent into the barn, and went to see how it fared with her. The barn door was barred, so he climbed in through a window. What did he find? His sister Rosalie lying on the straw in a dead faint. Tenderly he took her in his arms, tenderly he carried her into his house. 'Oh see, my wife, see, see, who it was we turned from our door last night!'

Now his wife, too, was all tenderness. Together they put wine to Rosalie's pale lips, wrapped her in blankets, and carried her to bed. And when she had come to herself, Rosalie told them her sad story.

'I will not eat, I will not drink, I will not sleep in my bed again, until I have killed that Ubir!' cried Sidor.

And he went to rouse his brothers.

'We will none of us eat, we will none of us drink, we will none of us sleep in our beds again, until we have killed that Ubir!' cried Vanka and Yury. And they all three saddled their horses, took their guns, and rode off to the forest where Ubir had her dwelling.

They tethered their horses on a grass plat, and went into the forest, keeping a sharp look-out, and dodging from tree to tree. And in a clearing under a mighty oak, they found Ubir, sprawled in sleep.

Cautiously they climbed up into the oak, cautiously they leaned from the branches, cautiously took aim, and all three fired their bullets down upon Ubir's hideous head.

Ubir woke with a roar of laughter. 'Oh ho, my breakfasts! I see you, my breakfasts! Come down, come down, my breakfasts!'

She seized the oak in her huge arms. The oak rocked, the oak groaned, the brothers fired their bullets again and again – they might as well have been firing crumbs of bread. Ubir opened her great mouth, swallowed down the bullets, smacked her lips, bellowed with laughter. Now she had pulled up the oak by the roots, now she was cramming it, roots first, into her mouth. Tree, brothers, and all, soon would be inside her great stomach.

'This is the end!' cried Vanka. 'Oh, for a silver bullet to pierce the monster's brain!'

Then Sidor remembered that he had a silver coin in his pocket. Would that do? He could but try! He put the coin into the muzzle of his gun: he fired. What happened? Ubir fell to the ground, the brothers crashed on top of her. . . . But they were alive, and Ubir was dead. So they left her lying, and rode home to tell Rosalie the glad tidings.

And when they had all rejoiced together, Rosalie said goodbye to her brothers and their wives, and went back to her own cottage, where her little horse was the only living soul to welcome her. But she didn't stay there lonely for very long. She married a young squire, and with him lived happily to the end of her days.

2 · Monster Copper Forehead

Once upon a time a man called Zar put some food in his wallet, and went into the forest to hunt for game. He hunted here, he hunted there, he found no game, he wandered in the forest for days and days. Now he had no more food, and he was hungry. Thinks he, 'I must go home before I starve.'

And he turned to go home.

Then came a roaring from behind the trees, and out sprang huge Monster Copper Forehead.

Zar raised his gun, and fired.

Bah! The bullet bounced off Monster Copper Forehead like a stone thrown against a wall.

'Now I shall eat you!' roared Monster Copper Forehead.

'Oh, oh, don't eat me, Monster Copper Forehead! Spare my life, and I will give you all I have!'

'Will you give me what you don't know you have at home?'

'Oh, oh, gladly, Monster Copper Forehead.'

'Very well, I will come for it tomorrow.'

Then Monster Copper Forehead went off, and Zar hurried home.

His wife was sitting by the hearth with a new-born baby boy on her lap.

'See, see, Zar! See what God has given us!'

And she held up the baby for Zar to kiss.

But Zar burst into tears. 'Not ours, not ours, the baby is not ours!' he wept.

'Why, mercy on us, whose else should he be?'

'Oh, oh! He belongs to Monster Copper Forehead!'

And he told her what had happened in the forest.

Now they were both weeping, and only the baby laughed and crowed.

Next morning – *bang, bang, bang!* There was Monster Copper Forehead at the door.

Zar's wife ran with the baby up into the loft. Zar opened the door.

'I have come for what you promised me,' roars Monster Copper Forehead.

'Oh, Monster Copper Forehead, oh your majesty, don't carry away our baby, not today, Monster Copper Forehead! Let us keep him, if but for a little while, Monster Copper Forehead! We love him so much, so much! I will give you everything else I possess, Monster Copper Forehead!'

'Bah!' said Monster Copper Forehead. 'What else *do* you possess? Nothing at all! Stand up on your feet, you stupid fellow! If I let you keep him until he is twelve years old, will you swear to let me have him then?'

'Oh yes, yes, yes, Monster Copper Forehead!'

'It will be the worse for you if you do not,' said Monster Copper Forehead. Then he strode off, and Zar's wife came down from the loft with the baby.

They called the baby Ivan, they loved him dearly. And as the years passed they loved him more and more. He was a strong handsome little lad, well worth anyone's loving. But who can hold back the years? Now Ivan was ten years old, now he was eleven years old, now his twelfth birthday was drawing near.

'Monster Copper Forehead shall not have him!' said Zar.

'No, no, Monster Copper Forehead shall *not*!' said Zar's wife.

So what did they do? Zar fetched his old mother and put her to live in his house. And he built a huge cellar at the bottom of his garden, and stocked it well with food. The cellar had a trap door. Zar took his wife and Ivan, went down into the cellar, and locked the trap door above them. And there they lived.

Now there was nobody in the house except Zar's old mother. And if Monster Copper Forehead came seeking, she was to know nothing – oh, nothing at all.

Well, on the very day that was Ivan's twelfth birthday, sure enough, there was Monster Copper Forehead banging at Zar's door. *Bang, bang, bang!*

Zar's old mother opened the door.

'Good morrow to you, little grandmother. Anyone else at home?'

'No, no one but myself, Monster Copper Forehead.'

'Then where is Zar? And where is Zar's wife, and where is little lad Ivan?'

'Dear me, they went out, Monster Copper Forehead. They went out, and they haven't come back. I don't know where they can be!'

'Little grandmother, don't you lie to me. If you lie to me it will be the worse for you. I have been known to make my dinner off little old grandmothers.'

'Oh! Oh! Oh! Don't eat me, Monster Copper Forehead. If a poor old woman has given her promise, what can a poor old woman do? No, no, I can't tell you anything. But take the poker out into the garden. Give it a toss. Maybe it will tell you where they are, Monster Copper Forehead.'

So Monster Copper Forehead picked up the poker and went out into the garden. He balanced the poker on a great forefinger, and said:

> '*Ivan, mother and father Zar,*
> *Poker, show me where they are.*'

Then he tossed the poker into the air; and it fell down on a flag-stone, exactly above the trap door.

Monster Copper Forehead stooped and scratched up the flag-stone with his long nails. Then he set to work on the trap door, and had it open quicker than quick. He put his huge horny hand into the cellar, feeling here, feeling there. No good your creeping into corners, Ivan, mother, and father Zar, Monster Copper Forehead's groping fingers close on you in no time; kick and struggle as you will, he's got you, and he's pulled you out, all three of you.

'And if I weren't a kind-hearted fellow,' roared Monster Copper Forehead, 'I'd crack your skull in, Zar, for so deceiving me!'

Then he tossed Zar and Zar's wife into a flower bed, and strode off with Ivan to his house in the dark forest.

In that house Monster Copper Forehead had a little girl, called Berta, whom he had taken from an unkind stepmother; because, though he was a monster, and a rough one, he loved children. He fed and tended the two children well, only he would never let them go out of the house, lest they run away from him, and that made them unhappy.

But one day, when Monster Copper Forehead was out hunting hares, there came Greatest-of-All Ravens flying round the house.

'*Kruk! Kruk!* Young Ivan! *Kruk! Kruk!* Little Berta! Sit yourselves on my back, and I will carry you home.'

'Oh, dear Raven, we can't get out! The door is locked and the windows are barred.'

'*Kruk! Kruk!* Creep up the chimney, young Ivan. Creep up the chimney, little Berta!'

So the children climbed up the chimney, and Greatest-of-All Ravens perched on the roof. The children clambered on to his back, and away he flew.

So, when Monster Copper Forehead comes home – see there, the children are gone!

Monster Copper Forehead wastes no time. He runs out of the house, he rolls his great eyes this way and that way, up at the sky, down across the earth. He sees Greatest-of-All Ravens flying far off towards the east. He stamps with his huge foot, and up from the ground shoots a long-reaching flame of fire. The flame, blown by Monster Copper Forehead's mighty breath, rises high into the air, and bends itself to eastward. It overtakes Greatest-of-All Ravens, it licks his wings. Greatest-of-All Ravens falls to earth, the children tumble off his back. Monster Copper Forehead runs, he gives Greatest-of-All Ravens a kick that sends him spinning. He picks up young Ivan, he picks up little Berta, and carries them both back to his house.

'Oh, you naughty, naughty children – now you shall have nothing but bread and water for your supper!'

Another day, when Monster Copper Forehead was out hunting, there came Great Long-Winged Falcon flying over the house.

'*Hek-hek-hek!* Young Ivan! *Hek-hek-hek-ek!* Little Berta! Why are you moping indoors on this beautiful morning?'

'Oh, dear Long-Winged Falcon, Monster Copper Forehead has bolted the door and barred the window. We can't get out!'

'Creep up the chimney, young Ivan. Creep up the chimney, little Berta, and I will carry you home.'

So the children crept up the chimney. And Long-Winged Falcon took them on his back and flew off with them.

Monster Copper Forehead comes back. What, no children! He rolls his great eyes here, there, everywhere. He sees Long-Winged Falcon with the children on his back, flying away to the west. He stamps with his great foot, up shoots the long-reaching flame of fire. He blows with his mighty breath, the flame rises high into the air, it bends to the west, it overtakes Long-Winged Falcon, it singes his wings. Long-Winged Falcon falls to the ground, the children tumble off his back, Monster Copper Forehead runs, picks up both children in his great fist, and carries them home.

'Naughty, naughty children! Tonight you shall have no supper – not even bread and water!'

Well, well, for some days after that Monster Copper Forehead didn't leave the house, so worried was he about the children trying to escape. But there came a day when he must go out to hunt for meat. And no sooner was he out of sight than White-Horned Bull came strolling by and peered through the window.

'*Moo-oo*, young Ivan! *Moo-oo*, little Berta. Why are you sitting indoors on this bright morning?'

'Oh, dear White-Horned Bull, we sit indoors because we can't get out. The door is locked, the window is barred, the chimney is blocked up.'

'Well, well, young Ivan, well, well, little Berta, break a window pane and come. I will take you on my back and carry you home.'

'Dear White-Horned Bull, if Greatest-of-All Ravens couldn't take us, and Long-Winged Falcon couldn't take us – how can you carry us home?'

'I can and I will! I can run faster than the wind blows. Come!'

So young Ivan picked up the poker and smashed a window pane.

And the children both clambered through the broken window and got on to the back of White-Horned Bull.

Then off galloped White-Horned Bull, faster than the wind blows.

Monster Copper Forehead came home. What, what, the window pane broken, and the children gone! Monster Copper Forehead roared in his rage: sky and earth echoed with his roaring. He rolled his great eyes here, there, everywhere. Far away across the plain he saw a flash of Bull's white horns as he went galloping, galloping. But White-Horned Bull was too far off for Monster Copper Forehead's flaming breath to reach him. With thunderous roar after thunderous roar, Monster Copper Forehead set off in pursuit.

White-Horned Bull was galloping, galloping. Monster Copper Forehead was racing, racing. But what now? Before White-Horned Bull there lies a wide water, stretching fathoms deep from one side of the plain to the other side. No way round! White-Horned Bull has never learned to swim. If he plunges into that wide water he will be drowned, and young Ivan will be drowned, and little Berta will be drowned. And behind them Master Copper Forehead, racing with long strides, is coming nearer and nearer. What to do? Oh, what to do?

'I can but fight and die,' says White-Horned Bull.

But no, see! Across the Wide Water on a strong raft, come Sharp-Clawed Cat and Bristle-Haired Dog, sturdily rowing. 'Jump on to our raft, White-Horned Bull, jump on to our raft, young Ivan, jump on to our raft, little Berta; we will carry you across the Wide Water!'

So White-Horned Bull and young Ivan and little Berta scramble on to the raft, and Sharp-Clawed Cat and Bristle-Haired Dog row them over the Wide Water. And above their heads come flying Greatest-of-All Ravens and Long-Winged Falcon, whose singed feathers have now grown again.

'*Kruk! Kruk! Hek-hek-he-ek! Hip, hip, hurr-a-ah!* Are we not a merry party? Away, and away, and away we go, over the Wide Water!'

Bellowing with rage Monster Copper Forehead comes to the edge of the Wide Water. He stamps with his huge foot, and over the Wide Water shoots a long-reaching flame of fire. But his stamping sets the

Wide Water a-shiver with waves, the waves rise up and drench the flame of fire; and beyond the waves, where the water is calm, the raft floats rapidly on.

If White-Horned Bull had never learned to swim, neither has Monster Copper Forehead. He wades into the Wide Water up to his chin, up to his mouth, up to his nose. If he takes another step he will be drowned. Shedding bitter tears Monster Copper Forehead wades back out of the Wide Water, and returns to his lonely house.

On the other side of the Wide Water Sharp-Clawed Cat and Bristle-Haired Dog lived in a little hut. To this hut they brought Ivan and Berta and Raven and Falcon and White-Horned Bull. And there they all lived together merrily for some time. But in his lonely house Monster Copper Forehead mourned, and often and often he would come across the plain to stand on the shore of the Wide Water. And there he would stretch out his great hairy arms and cry, 'Come back, come back, young Ivan! Come back, come back to me, little Berta!' And the wind carried the sound of his crying over the Wide Water and round the walls of the little hut, where Ivan and Berta and Falcon and Raven and White-Horned Bull lived with Sharp-Clawed Cat and Bristle-Haired Dog.

'Oh, poor Monster Copper Forehead, how sad he is!' said little Berta. 'Hark to his moaning!'

'Bah! Let him moan!' said young Ivan.

'But he was kind to us, and I cannot bear it!' said little Berta.

No, Berta couldn't bear to think of Monster Copper Forehead's misery. And one day, when Ivan and Cat and Dog and Raven and Falcon and White-Horned Bull had all gone hunting, she went down to the shore, got on the raft, rowed it across the Wide Water, and found Monster Copper Forehead standing knee deep in the water on the opposite shore, and shedding fiery tears that set the little waves hissing and sparkling.

'Ah, ah, you will come back and live with me, my darling!' cried Monster Copper Forehead.

'No,' said little Berta. 'But get on the raft, and I will take you to live with us.'

So Monster Copper Forehead got on to the raft, and Berta rowed him over the Wide Water, and brought him to the empty hut. And there she set meat and drink before him and said, 'Now we can all be happy!'

'I do not think so,' said Monster Copper Forehead. 'When young Ivan returns there will be trouble.'

'But you must promise not to hurt him, Monster Copper Forehead!'

And Monster Copper Forehead answered, 'For your sake I will not hurt a hair of his head, little Berta.'

Now soon came the sound of merry voices outside: Ivan and Cat and Dog and Raven and Falcon and White-Horned Bull returning from the hunt. They were singing a song about how they were going to shoot Monster Copper Forehead with their bows and arrows, should he venture across the Wide Water.

Berta was frightened. 'Oh, Monster Copper Forehead, where can I hide you?'

What did Master Copper Forehead do then? He stamped with his huge foot; he snapped with his great fingers. He turned himself into a pin. And Berta stuck the pin into the wall.

In came Ivan and Cat and Dog and Raven and Falcon and White-Horned Bull.

'Berta, is the oven hot? Is the kettle boiling? We have game to cook.'

'Yes, Ivan, the oven is hot, and the kettle is boiling.'

Ivan sat down, Raven and Falcon and White-Horned Bull sat down. But what were Cat and Dog doing? Dog was running round the room, sniffing and growling. Cat was leaping at the wall, sniffing and mie-owling.

'*Gr-rr-gr-rr!* There's something here that shouldn't be here,' growled Dog.

'*Mieow-ow-ow!* There's *certainly* something here that shouldn't be here!'

But Ivan got cross, and told them to sit down. And at last they did sit down, and they all had supper.

Next morning they went out to hunt again. Berta took the pin out of the wall. The pin gave a jerk and changed itself into Monster Copper Forehead.

'Oh, Monster Copper Forehead, dear Monster Copper Forehead,' cried Berta. 'You must go back home, or there will be murder done!'

But Monster Copper Forehead shed fiery tears. 'I will *not* go back to my lonely house,' he sobbed.

'Then I will come with you, Monster Copper Forehead.'

'And stay with me?' said Monster Copper Forehead.

'Yes, why not?' said Berta. 'But you must never again lock the door and bar the window and keep me prisoner.'

'I will never, never keep you prisoner again, dear little Berta!'

So Berta rowed Monster Copper Forehead back over the Wide Water, and went to live with him in his house in the forest. And Ivan said, 'Oh, botheration! Berta has run away, and we have lost our housekeeper. Now we must take it in turns to stay at home and do the cooking!'

But they never again heard the sound of Monster Copper Forehead's voice, crying and moaning across the Wide Water. And that was a great relief. So they lived in contentment, until one day Ivan thought about his parents and said, 'I think I ought to go and see what is happening at home – but I don't like to go empty-handed.'

'Well, you needn't go empty-handed,' said Cat. And she went to scratch under a tree outside the hut. 'Come and dig here,' said she.

So Cat scratched and Dog dug under the tree. They dug a big hole. And what did they find at the bottom of that hole? A chest full of gold pieces.

'Oh ho! Oh ho!' Ivan clapped his hands and shouted. Dog barked, Cat purred, Falcon and Raven flew round and round turning aerial somersaults, White-Horned Bull bellowed joyfully. Ivan roped the chest on to the back of White-Horned Bull, and off they set.

They travelled for days and days, they travelled east, they travelled west, they travelled north, they travelled south – they didn't know which road to take. But one day Long-Winged Falcon flew high up into the air, and looking this way and that over the world, his bright eyes spied a little cottage, tucked away in a valley beyond great forest trees.

'*Kek-kek-kek!* I see something, friend Ivan!'

26

'What is it you see, Long-Winged Falcon?'

'I see a little cottage, friend Ivan. An old man is digging in the garden, and an old woman sits at the door spinning. The old man has a nose like your nose, friend Ivan, and the old woman's smile is your smile. I think they must be your father and your mother!'

So they hastened, and came to the little house.

The old woman got up and curtseyed; the old man put down his spade and bowed.

'Welcome, strangers!'

'Well, perhaps not strangers! Is your name Zar and is this your wife?'

'Yes, my name is Zar, and this is my old woman.'

'Then good morning, dear father, and good morning, dear mother! I am Ivan, come home at last.'

Oh, what rejoicing! Son Ivan come home! Son Ivan come home after all these years! Old man Zar is shouting and laughing. Old Mrs Zar is weeping for joy. Ivan tells them all his story; he opens the big chest full of gold pieces. 'See, little father, see, little mother, your Ivan has not come home empty-handed! Now, little father, you can rest from your labours; now, little mother, your hands shall no more roughen themselves with scrubbing and scouring. Now you shall wear a velvet coat, little father; and you, little mother, shall have a gown of silk. Now we will pull down this poor cottage and build us a lordly house.'

And that's what they did. They built their lordly house. They were happy, oh, so happy! Zar wore a velvet coat, Mrs Zar wore a gown of silk. Cat slept on a satin cushion; Dog wore a silver collar. Ivan wooed the lovely daughter of a count, and married her, and brought her home. White-Horned Bull lorded it in the home meadows over a herd of meek-eyed cows. Greatest-of-All Ravens and Long-Winged Falcon found mates, and built nests in the garden. And Monster Copper Forehead never came to singe their feathers. Why should Monster Copper Forehead bother himself about Ivan and his friends? Monster Copper Forehead had Berta to keep house for him – what more did he need?

But Berta was growing up. She was no longer *little Berta*, she was

a tall and beautiful maiden. And this tall and beautiful maiden was sometimes very sad.

But when Monster Copper Forehead asked her what ailed her, she only shook her head and said, 'I don't know.'

'But *I* know,' said Monster Copper Forehead. 'Oh, oh, *I* know! And though it break my heart, I will make you happy!'

Then Monster Copper Forehead ran out of the house. He left Berta alone all day, and when he came back in the evening he was carrying a young prince under his arm.

'There,' said he, setting the prince down in front of Berta, 'what did I tell you? Isn't she good? Isn't she beautiful? Doesn't she shine like the very sun, doesn't she, *doesn't she*?'

'She makes the darkness bright about her,' said the prince.

Berta laughed. She knew now what had made her sad; and she knew now what would make her happy. So when the prince asked her if she would be his wife, she said, 'Yes, oh, yes!'

Then Monster Copper Forehead tucked Berta under one arm, and the prince under the other arm, strode off with them to the prince's palace, and set them down at the gate.

'I will not come in to fright the wedding guests,' he said. 'I will say goodbye to you here, my little Berta.'

'Oh, Monster Copper Forehead,' cried Berta, 'you have been so kind to me, you have given me so much, so much! What can I give you in return?'

'One kiss?' said Monster Copper Forehead, stooping low.

So Berta stood on the tips of her toes and kissed his coppery cheek. . . .

Then Monster Copper Forehead went back to his lonely house.

He was smiling to himself.

3 · The Golden Valley

A king had three sons, whom he loved beyond all measure. And indeed they deserved his love, for they were gallant, handsome fellows all three. And one day the king said to the eldest prince, whose name was Rosario, 'Son, tomorrow I am going to take a drive into the country, to view my realm. Will you come with me?'

'Yes, indeed I will!' said Rosario.

So next day the king and Rosario set out, driving in a splendid coach and followed by a retinue of knights and squires. They drove up hill and down dale, and under the mountains. And among the mountains they came into a green and flowery valley.

'Oh, Father,' said Rosario, 'how beautiful is this valley! Let us stay here and eat our midday meal!'

But the king said, 'I have a feeling that if we drive on we shall come to an even more beautiful place.'

So they drove on, and came into a bleak deserted valley, full of great boulders, and the ruins of old dwellings, and tall-growing thistles. And Rosario said, 'Oh, Father, we should have stayed in the other valley!'

But the king said, 'I have a feeling that we shall come to something better presently.'

So they drove on out of the bleak valley and over the crest of a hill, and came down into a third valley, where everything was gold. The mountains that sheltered the valley were gold, the stream that flowed through the valley was gold, the flowers were gold, the trees were gold, and every bird that sang among those trees had golden feathers.

'Oh, Father,' cried Rosario, 'how beautiful, how beautiful is this valley! Here I could live forever. Dear Father, do me a favour, grant my wish, build me a little house here in this valley – I do not wish to return to the city!'

'My son, are you crazy?' said the king. 'How could you live here, far from the court, and from me, and from your mother?'

But Rosario answered, 'Having seen this valley, I cannot, I will not live anywhere else!'

So the king, because he loved Rosario beyond all measure, sent to the city for masons and carpenters, and ordered them to build a little house in the golden valley. In three days the house was built, and well stocked with provisions. And Rosario took possession of it. No, he wouldn't have any servants there to wait on him: he was going to live a simple life, all by himself. So the king and the queen and the other two princes, who had come to view the house, drove back to the city.

'I don't much like this!' said the king to the queen. 'A prince, and heir to the throne, to live like a hermit in the desert.'

But the queen said, 'He will soon tire and come back to us. It is only a foolish fancy.'

'Yes, yes, only a foolish fancy!' said the king. And he cheered up.

Left alone, Rosario walked through every room of his little house, went to stand in the porch, looked this way and that way over the gleaming golden valley, and rejoiced. 'Now I am king indeed!' he said to himself. 'King of these golden mountains and this bright valley, and these beautiful flowers and birds! King over my own thoughts, with no one to trouble me, and no irksome duties filling up my every minute!'

So he spent a happy day, and after the sun had set, and the golden valley gleamed softly in the evening light, he cooked himself a simple meal, and went happily to bed.

And happily he slept until midnight. But then – *Bang! Crash!* A frightful noise! *Bang, crash, roar, boom!* The walls of the house shook, the floors heaved, the window panes fell in, the doors dropped from their hinges. Rosario was flung violently from his bed, and snatching a cloak he rushed out into the night – only just in time, for no sooner was he through the front door than the whole of the house fell down.

Now the valley and all the mountains that surrounded the valley echoed with huge shouts of laughter – and what was that *thing* coming towards Rosario? An immense monster, glittering all over with fiery sparks of gold! Rosario turned and fled, down through the valley, up over the mountains: he ran, ran, ran, with the monster's laughter booming in his ears, and the ground under the monster's feet heaving and cracking, and the golden trees crashing their boughs, and the wakened birds shrilly screaming.

It was indeed a crestfallen Rosario who arrived home late in the day, and told the king that the valley was bewitched, and that never, never would he set foot in it again.

The king thought that was a very good thing; but Giovanni, the second prince, said, 'Pooh! What a coward! A prince of the realm to be frightened by a thunderstorm! Oh, well, all right – a little earthquake, if you will, but that doesn't make it less shameful to be afraid, and to be making monsters out of moonlit shadows! Father, build *me* a little house in the valley, that I may prove to this hero-brother of mine how causeless his fears were!'

Well, the king was reluctant to do any such thing, but Giovanni bothered and bothered until the king agreed, and sent workmen again to the valley to build a second little house. And strange to say, when they came into the valley they found not a stone overturned or a tree uprooted; the valley glowed in its golden beauty as heretofore; only the wreckage of Rosario's house lay neatly piled where it had fallen.

'So you see,' said Prince Giovanni, 'it was merely a little earthquake, and earthquakes only happen once in a blue moon! Come, clear away this rubbish, my men, for I will have my house built just where my brother's was.'

So the workmen cleared away the rubbish and built another little house on the same spot. And when the house was ready, Prince Giovanni bade the king and the queen a laughing goodbye, said he would come back to visit them in a week's time, jumped on his horse, and rode off to the valley.

But he was back in less than a week, he was back next day, for exactly the same thing happened to him as had happened to Rosario: at midnight came the roaring and the crashing, and the falling in of the house, and the glittering monster, and the booming laughter, and Giovanni taking to his heels and fleeing through the night – not on his horse, but on his own feet, for the horse had broken his tether, and galloped home at the very first sound of that booming laughter.

'This is more than strange!' said the youngest prince, Cosmo. 'There must be some reason for all this! Father, build *me* a little house in the valley, and let me go there, for I cannot rest until I have solved this mystery.'

'Oh, my son,' said the king, 'isn't what has happened to your two brothers enough, but you must also go frightening yourself out of your wits, and risking your precious life? If the valley is haunted, it is haunted. Let well alone. I will have a high fence built at the entrance to the valley, and a notice placed there to warn all travellers.'

'Are we a race of cowards then, that we must put up with this indignity in our own kingdom?' cried Prince Cosmo. 'If you will not build me a house, I must do without one. But spend a night in that valley I must, and will!'

So the king, seeing that there was no dissuading him, built Cosmo a little house; and when it was ready, ordered out his coach, and himself drove with Prince Cosmo to the golden valley, and there bade him goodbye, fully expecting to see him come running home next day as his brothers had done, 'if – oh dear! – nothing worse befall him!' thought the king, as he drove back to the palace.

Left alone, the prince spent a happy day, and when evening came, stoked up his fire, and cooked his supper. But he didn't go to bed; he lit his lamp and sat by the fire with a book, every now and then lifting his head and listening for any unusual sound. And so he sat till midnight.

And at midnight came – what? No bang, no crash, no heaving of floors, nor rattling of walls. Just a tramp of heavy feet outside, and then two huge round eyes, like two golden full moons, peering in through the window.

The prince got up, and opened the door. And there, towering up against the stars, stood the great monster, glittering all over with fiery sparks of gold.

'Ah, good evening!' said the prince. 'Pray come in!'

'Why aren't you in bed?' roared the monster, stooping to step through the door.

'I don't go to bed when I'm expecting a guest,' said Prince Cosmo. 'I stay up to welcome him.'

'Were you expecting *me*?' roared the monster.

'Most assuredly I was,' said the prince.

'And *do* you welcome me?' bellowed the monster.

'Most assuredly I do,' answered the prince.

'But . . . but . . .' bellowed the monster, 'aren't you afraid?'

'No,' said the prince. 'Why should I be?'

'Everyone else is,' said the monster.

'That's neither here nor there,' said the prince. 'But tell me – to what do I owe the pleasure of this visit?'

The monster seemed a bit taken aback. He was silent for a moment, then he shouted, 'It *isn't* a pleasure! It *oughtn't* to be a pleasure! I could kill you with a breath!'

'Well, I don't think you will,' said the prince. 'What harm have I done you?'

'What harm?' roared the monster. 'What harm? You come here putting up your gim-crack little house in my beautiful valley, and you ask me *what harm!*'

'*Your* valley?' said Prince Cosmo. 'You must pardon me, but I thought the valley belonged to the king, my father.'

'Well, it doesn't,' said the monster. 'It belongs to *me!* It belonged to me before your father, or your father's father, or your father's father's father, were born. It's my home! *Mine!* It was my home before any of you mannikins existed on earth! And here you come messing it up with your lath and plaster, after all the trouble I've taken to make it pretty!'

'And it certainly is very pretty,' said the prince.

'Yes, isn't it?' said the monster with a grin. Then he scowled. 'But now I must kill you! What shall we do – fight?'

'As you will,' said Prince Cosmo. 'I have my sword here, and I'll do my best. But I expect you could kill me with one blow of your great golden fist.'

'That's just it,' said the monster, 'I could. And it wouldn't be fair; I should like to fight fair. Besides you're a brave lad – it would be a pity to kill you.'

'Well, then,' said the prince, 'there are other ways of fighting. What about a contest of wits?'

'Wits – what's wits?' said the monster.

'Well, brains then,' said the prince.

'Oh, the things we think with,' said the monster. 'How can we fight with *them*?'

'We could ask riddles,' said the prince. 'If I guess your riddles, and you can't guess mine – I win. And contrariwise, if I can't guess your riddles – you win.'

The monster grinned and slapped his thigh with his great fist, making the house shake. 'Oh, I know some lovely riddles – riddles you'll never guess!' he shouted.

'Well, you begin,' said the prince.

'Then this is my first riddle,' said the monster. 'What runs without feet?'

The prince thought that was a very easy riddle. But in order to please the monster, he hesitated before answering – screwed up his eyes, tapped his chin with his forefinger, and at last said, 'Can it be a river by any chance?'

'Right!' roared the monster. 'Aren't you clever!'

'I have been told so,' said the prince modestly. 'And your second riddle?'

'At night they come without being fetched. And by day they are lost without being stolen,' roared the monster. 'That one will fox you!'

'Indeed I think it will!' said the prince. And again he pretended to think. 'Could it possibly be stars?' he asked, after a while.

'Right again, clever mannikin!' shouted the monster. 'Two to you! But the third you won't guess in a hurry!'

'Well, let's have it,' said the prince.

'I ran and got it,' said the monster. 'I sat and I searched for it.

If I could get it, I would not bring it with me. But as I couldn't get it, I had to carry it along with me.'

'My word!' said the prince. 'That is indeed a poser!'

'Give up?' said the monster.

'No, no,' said the prince. 'I must think, I must think!'

'Think away,' said the monster. 'We've got the night before us.'

'I ran and I got it,' murmured the prince. 'I sat and I searched for it – it can't be anything very nice, or I wouldn't mind bringing it along with me. Ah! Do you know I really think it must be a thorn in the foot!'

'That's just what it is,' said the monster.

'Then that's three to me,' said the prince.

'Ye-es,' said the monster. 'And it's a bitter blow, I can tell you! I never thought you'd guess that last one.'

'Cheer up!' said the prince. 'I expect you'll just as easily guess mine. And here's the first:

> 'Formed long ago, yet made today,
> I stand whilst others sleep,
> What few would wish to give away,
> Nor any wish to keep.'

The monster thought and thought; he frowned, shut his golden eyes, opened them again, grunted, grinned, frowned again. He had no idea of the answer. The prince wanted to help him, so he yawned, crossed the room, went to curl up on the sofa. 'I don't think I'm going to get much sleep tonight,' he murmured 'though this sofa would make a comfortable enough *bed.*'

'It's a bed, a bed, the answer is a bed!' roared the monster.

'So it is,' said the prince. 'And aren't *you* clever! Now for the second riddle:

> 'From house to house he goes,
> A traveller, small and slight.
> And whether it rains or snows,
> He sleeps outside in the night.'

'I can guess that one!' cried the monster. 'It's a little road!'

'You're right,' said the prince. 'Clever of you!'

'Well,' said the monster, 'to tell the truth I've heard it before. So I suppose it doesn't count?'

'Oh, it counts all right,' said the prince. 'And here's the third:

'When I wore my white skirt
No one wanted me.
When I put on my green cap,
No one would have me.
When I wore my red jacket,
Few wanted me.
But when I put on my black suit
Everyone wanted me.'

'You do make them difficult,' growled the monster. 'But I think the answer must be a sweetheart.'

'No, it isn't,' said the prince. 'Who ever wanted a sweetheart in a black suit?'

'Well, then, a coach to ride in?'

'Wrong again,' said the prince. 'I'd rather ride in a green coach than a black one any day!'

'A black suit, a black suit! Who wears a black suit?' said the monster. 'Ah, I have it – a parson!'

'Well, some people may want a parson,' said the prince. 'But I don't think *everybody* does. Moreover I've never seen a parson running about in a green cap, nor yet in a red jacket. Now, you've had your three guesses!'

'But maybe you don't know the answer yourself?' said the monster.

'Oh yes I do,' said the prince. 'It's a blackberry. *And I've won!*'

'So you have,' said the monster. 'But I don't see how you're going to kill me.'

'*Kill* you! Why should I want to kill you?'

'Well,' said the monster, 'wasn't that what the contest was for? To decide which one of us should kill the other?'

'Certainly not!' said the prince. 'It was just to decide whether or not I might keep my house here in the valley.'

'So it was!' said the Monster. 'And now I suppose you must keep it. But oh – oh – it's such an *ugly* house!'

'Is it?' said the prince. 'I thought it was rather pretty.'

'It is *not* pretty,' wailed the monster. 'It's a blot on my golden valley! It's ugly, *ugly!* UGLY!'

'Well then, big clever boy,' said the prince, 'make it prettier.'

'Shall I?' said the monster. 'Shall I? Yes, I will! Here, you get out of the way! Give me room!'

So the prince went to stand outside in the moonlight, well away from the house. And the monster blew on his great fingers, and went from room to room inside the house, touching everything. And whatever he touched – whether the walls, or the furniture, or the pots and pans, or the plates and dishes and drinking cups – turned to glistening gold. Then he came outside, and stroked the roof and the chimneys and the walls, and they too turned to gold. It was a pretty sight when he had done with it, was that little house, gleaming softly in the moonlight.

'Now that's as it should be,' said the monster to the prince. 'And *you* are as you should be. I like you! I like you better than any human being I have ever come across!'

'Have you come across many?' asked the prince.

'A good few,' said the monster. 'Puny little creatures that squall and run when they catch sight of a body. But you didn't squall, and you didn't run. And that's why I like you.'

'Well,' said the prince, 'you are the first monster I have ever met. And certainly I can say I like you.'

'And you're not a bit afraid of me,' shouted the monster.

But the prince did feel rather alarmed when the monster picked him up and gave him a hug. For that hug nearly squeezed the breath out of his body; though to be sure it was the gentlest hug the monster knew how to give.

'Steady, big boy, steady!' gasped the prince. 'As you so rightly said, we are but puny!'

'Oh, I forgot,' said the monster. 'It was joy because you said you liked me. But I won't do it again.' Then he gave a tremendous yawn. 'Think I'll go to bed now.'

'Where do you sleep?' asked the prince.

'*Ha, ha, ha!* Shan't tell you!' laughed the monster.

And he strode away up the valley.

The prince laughed also, and went to bed. He slept late, and when he woke next morning he wondered whether all the happenings of the night before had been a dream. But no! There was his little house glowing golden in the morning light. So he jumped out of bed and dressed. He felt very happy.

But back in the royal palace the king, his father, and the queen, his mother, waited anxiously. They were expecting every moment to see their youngest son come fleeing home in terror, as his brothers had done. And as the hours went by and he did not return, they became more and more anxious.

'We should never have let him go!' wailed the queen. 'Perhaps even now he is lying dead under the ruins of his fallen house! Or perhaps that terrible monster may have struck him on the head and killed him!'

So then the king called for his coach, and he and the queen and Prince Rosario and Prince Giovanni drove off to the golden valley, accompanied by a regiment of soldiers. And when they reached the valley – what did they see? Prince Cosmo's little house glittering gold in the noonday light, and Prince Cosmo himself standing at the door, scattering crumbs for a flock of birds that surrounded him with merry chirruping and the flutter of golden wings.

'Oh, my dear son, my dear, dear son, you are safe and well!' cried the queen.

'Why – what else should I be?' said Prince Cosmo.

'But – but the monster – didn't he come?' asked Prince Rosario.

'Yes, he came,' answered Cosmo. 'We got on very well together. I found him a pleasant fellow. He didn't like the look of my house, so he set about improving it, as you see. He's a grand monster, truly he is, and I look forward to seeing him again.'

'But you will come home with us now?' said the queen.

'I think I would rather stay here for a while,' said Prince Cosmo. 'I am only a younger son, I am not needed at court, and I am looking forward to more visits from my monster. He can teach me a lot of things.'

'*Teach you things!*' said the queen. 'What sort of things?'

'Things about monsters,' said Prince Cosmo. 'They must be an interesting race. No, I don't mean to come back until I've learned more about them.'

So, since there was no persuading Prince Cosmo to return with them, the king and the queen and Prince Rosario and Prince Giovanni, and the regiment of soldiers went back to the court.

Now there was Prince Cosmo left alone in his golden house in the golden valley, and every evening the monster came stalking down the valley to visit him. The monster had many interesting things to tell the prince about monsters in general, and about the days before any human beings lived on earth, for he was millions and millions of years old. But what the monster liked best was asking and guessing riddles. And one evening he said, 'I've thought of a new riddle – a beauty! It's this: what makes the world to shine?'

'You,' said the prince. 'You, with your golden touch?'

'Pah!' said the monster. 'I mean *real* brightness.'

'Well – the sun then?'

'No,' said the monster, 'that's not the answer.'

The prince guessed this, that, and the other: but always the monster said 'No!' and 'No!' and 'No!' So at last the prince said, 'I give up. What *is* the answer?'

'A good friend,' said the monster, with a shout of triumph. '*And I've got one!*'

4 · *Lu-bo-bo*

The monster Gogo was a huge hairy monster, and a greedy monster. He was always over-eating; and when his stomach was too full and gave him pains, Gogo would grumble and say to his stomach:

> '*Let me alone, lu-bo-bo!*
> *Let me alone, lu-bo-bo!*'

But he went on eating all the same.

Every living thing on earth was food for greedy Gogo; and by night he came out of a cave underground and wandered through the country seeking what people or what animals he might devour.

Now you must know that there was a widow woman who had an only daughter, called Ayissa; and these two lived in a lonely cottage among fields, with no near neighbours. So in order to defend herself and her daughter against Gogo, the widow kept four great dogs, very strong, very fierce, very clever. The names of these four dogs were Shato, Fari, Samanduna, and Samanbussa. And every day the widow cooked for them a big dinner of roast meat and oatmeal porridge; and every evening she said to them, 'Keep good watch, my dogs, through the night, lest Monster Gogo comes this way.'

And the four dogs wagged their tails and said, 'Yes, yes, little mother, we'll keep watch. You go to bed and sleep without fear.'

And they did keep watch. When Gogo came wandering that way at night, seeking whom he might devour, and talking to his stomach, the four dogs set up such a fierce growling and such a furious barking that Gogo passed on. And so the widow and Ayissa lived in safety.

But one day the widow must go to town to buy provisions. And it was a long way to the town, so she decided to stay overnight with her cousins there. And before she set out she said to Ayissa, 'Don't forget the dogs' dinner. Roast the meat in good time, cook plenty of porridge, and fill their drinking pail with clean fresh well water. Remember all these things that you may sleep secure.'

And Ayissa answered, 'Yes, of course I'll remember – no need to remind me about *that!*'

So the widow set off for town. And Ayissa put the dogs' joint of meat in the oven, and their porridge to cook on the top of the stove. And after that, she bustled about with a broom and a duster, setting the house tidy.

And all at once the four dogs, who were lying outside in the shadow of the house, began to bark: not with angry barks, but with little welcoming ones.

'Ayissa! Ayissa!' Girls' voices were calling! Ayissa threw down her broom and ran to the door. There were four girl friends of hers come to visit her, and bringing some sweetmeats with them, and a bottle of wine.

In they all came, skipping and laughing: and sniff, sniff, sniff went their pretty little noses. 'O-oo, Ayissa, what's cooking? O-oo, doesn't it smell good! And aren't we hungry! Let's have a taste, Ayissa, let's have a taste!'

'Well,' said Ayissa, 'I expect you can have just a little taste. But it's really the evening food for the dogs.'

'Food for the dogs, then we'll be dogs!' cried the girls. '*Bow-wow-wow-wow!*' And there they were, jumping round the kitchen pretending to be dogs. But outside in the shadow of the house, Shato said to Fari, 'Silly things!' And Fari said to Shato, 'Well, well, they're but young.' And Samanduna said, 'Time they grew up then!' And Samanbussa said, 'Let them play whilst they may, as long as they don't eat up all our dinner!'

But that's just what the girls did. They ate all the meat, except for a few frizzled bits of fat; and they ate all the porridge except for the scrapings of the pot; they finished off with the sweetmeats and the wine they had themselves brought, and vowed they had never eaten a better dinner.

And after dinner, it was chit-chat and plenty of laughter, and teasing each other about the village lads, and gay nonsense. It was already late in the afternoon when they said goodbye to Ayissa, and scampered away to get safe home before dusk, lest the prowling Gogo catch them unawares. And it was only after they had gone that Ayissa remembered that the dogs had not had their dinner.

Goodness me! Oh, botheration! Well then – what was left? No porridge, no roast meat, except a few bits of fat and an overdone hard scrap or two that the girls had left on their plates. There wasn't any more meat in the house; and truly Ayissa told herself that she was tired out, and couldn't go making more porridge at this time of day. So the dogs would have to be satisfied for once with the bits and pieces she could scrape together. Tiresome spoiled creatures! And as to drinking water – botheration again! The water pails were empty – and how could she go out to the well, with twilight coming on, and that frightful Gogo most likely already on the prowl?

Shato, Fari, Samanduna and Samanbussa – there they all were now, crowding up the kitchen, wagging their tails and looking at her with expectant eyes.

'Here you are,' said Ayissa, setting down the dish of bits and pieces in front of them.

'*What!*' said Shato.

'Is that *our* dinner?' said Fari.

'It's not enough to feed a mouse!' said Samanduna.

'And where's the porridge?' said Samanbussa.

'Take it or leave it,' said Ayissa. 'My, I'm tired!' And she sat down and yawned.

'Seems we'll have to go and find our own dinner,' said Shato.

'Maybe farmer Salem will have something for us,' said Fari.

'Yes, yes, he's a kind man, we'll go and ask *him*,' said Samanduna.

'But we'll come back as soon as we can,' said Samanbussa. And off they all raced, out of the house and down the road to the nearest farm – and that was some way off.

All quiet in the cottage. Ayissa sat by the fire and yawned. She thought she would go to bed. Then she thought she had better wait till the dogs came back. Then she smiled to herself, and patted her smooth shining hair, thinking of something one of the girls had said about a lad in the village who admired her.

'But I don't intend to get married for a long time, so he'll just have to wait,' she said to herself. And she smiled again. . . .

But what was that sound outside? The garden gate creaking, a *flump, flump,* of heavy feet on the garden path: a voice loudly muttering:

> '*Let me alone, lu-bo-bo!*
> *Let me alone, lu-bo-bo!*'

GOGO!

Terrified, Ayissa sprang to the house door and bolted it; terrified she rushed upstairs into her bedroom and locked that door. But, *Crash!* – the house door is down, there's a trampling in the kitchen, a loud snuffling, a picking up and flinging down of empty dishes, and a wailing voice:

> '*Let me alone, lu-bo-bo!*
> *Let me alone, lu-bo-bo!*'

Footsteps on the stairs, a huge snuffling, a banging at the bedroom door, and still that wailing voice:

> '*Let me alone, lu-bo-bo!*
> *Let me alone, lu-bo-bo!*'

Ayissa was standing on the bed now, she was reaching up to a trap door in the ceiling, she had the trap door open, she was clambering through it into the loft, she was crouching down behind some old trunks. . . . But now Gogo had smashed down the bedroom door, now he was in the bedroom, now he was clambering on to the bed, now he was poking his hairy great head through the trap door, and still he was grumbling at his stomach:

> '*Let me alone, lu-bo-bo!*
> *Let me alone, lu-bo-bo!*'

And Ayissa, trembling and sobbing, was scrambling out of the loft window, and down into the yard.

44

In the yard was a great earthenware pot; Ayissa jumped into it, drew down the lid and crouched there, with her heart thumping against her ribs.

Sniff, snuffle, sniff, snuffle: Gogo was climbing out of the loft window, he was in the yard, he was sniffing at the earthenware pot. 'Ah ha! My good little supper!' Gogo took up the pot in his great hairy hands, he opened his great mouth, now the pot was in his mouth, and now he had swallowed down pot, Ayissa and all.

'You'll regret this,' said Gogo's stomach, as the pot came flumping down into it. 'I'm full to bursting, I tell you, full to bursting!'

But Gogo only answered, 'Let me alone, lu-bo-bo!' and wandered off across the fields in the gathering twilight, snatching up every living thing he met with, whether man or beast, and swallowing them down, heedless of his protesting stomach.

Now up the road from farmer Salem's, Shato and Fari and Samanduna and Samanbussa, tails up, ears pricked, full fed and joyous, came racing home.

But their ears fell flat, and their tails were tucked between their legs when they reached home. For in front of the broken house door stood Ayissa's mother, with her hands to her head and her eyes wild. 'Oh, oh, something told me I must come home, but this is worse than anything! Oh, oh, the house is a shambles – and where is Ayissa? Oh, oh, Gogo must have been here! Oh, oh, Gogo must have swallowed my little Ayissa! Oh, you bad wicked dogs! Oh, my little daughter, my little daughter! For this I will kill that Gogo!'

'Little mother, little mother, it is *we* who will kill that Gogo!' cried Shato, and Fari, and Samanduna, and Samanbussa. And off with them, tails up, noses to ground, *sniff, sniff, sniff*, darting this way, darting that way, following the scent of Gogo's footsteps, with the widow running behind them, waving a carving knife and sobbing.

Now the moon rose, round and full. Far ahead of them they could see the huge dark shape of Gogo ambling across the fields. Gogo was still grumbling at his stomach, but he wasn't looking for anything more to eat. He had such a very bad pain that he thought he would go to his cave and rest for a while. And he went to his cave and crawled into it, muttering:

'*Let me alone, lu-bo-bo!*
Let me alone, lu-bo-bo!'

And all at once Gogo's stomach screamed back at Gogo, 'I'm too full, I'm too full, I'm going to burst!'

And burst it did, with such a bang that Gogo, and cave, and all blew up. Nothing was left but a huge mound of grey stones and brown earth, and a tangle of long hairs.

Here then was the end of the trail! The four great dogs, Shato, and Fari, and Samanduna, and Samanbussa, came to the mount. *Sniff, sniff, sniff, sniff!* Now they were scrabbling at the mound with their front feet, burying their noses in the earth, tossing aside the earth, dragging away the stones: *sniff, sniff, sniff*, and *scrabble, scrabble, scrabble!*

And when they had made a deep hole in the mound, they sat back, ears pricked, tongues hanging out, and panting.

'Something's moving inside that hole!' said Shato.

'Yes, yes,' cried Fari, 'something's moving – and *something's coming out!*'

Something *was* coming out. It was a cock. With a dignified stride the cock stepped down over the tumbled stones and heaps of earth, stood for a moment blinking at the moon, flapped his wings and crowed, '*Erk-er-rik-oo!* I see the world!' Then he flapped his wings again, crowed again, and walked off across the fields.

'Somebody else is coming out!' said Samanduna.

'Yes, yes,' cried Samanbussa, 'somebody else is coming out!'

And out of the mound stepped a man.

The man rubbed his eyes, looked this way, looked that way.

'Ha!' said he. 'I see the world!'

And off he strode across the fields.

'Something else is coming out!' cried the four dogs.

And out of the mound scrambled a curly-haired dog.

'*Wow, wow, wow!*' cried the curly-haired dog. 'I see the world!'

And off he scampered after the man.

'Someone else is coming out!' cried Shato.

And out of the mound came a sharp-horned bull.

'*U-u-um!*' said the bull. 'I see the world!'

And he tossed his head, gave a sideways leap, and ran off across the fields.

'Someone else is coming out!' cried Fari.

And after the sharp-horned bull stepped out a goat.

'*May-ay-ay!*' cried the goat. 'I see the world!'

And off he ran across the fields.

And after the goat came out a little woolly lamb.

'*Ba-a-ah!*' cried the little woolly lamb. 'I see the world!'

And he gave a hop and a skip and scampered off across the fields.

And after the little woolly lamb came out a green-eyed cat. The cat looked up at the moon, and the moon glittered in her green eyes.

'*Miow-ow-ow!*' said the green-eyed cat. 'I see the world!'

And she walked off across the fields.

So it went on. The creatures were coming out of the mound one after another – there seemed no end to them. But where was the widow's little daughter, Ayissa – oh, where was she?

Hoping, despairing, now sobbing, now laughing, the widow stood by the hole in the ground. Surely, surely the next to come out would be Ayissa!

But Ayissa did not come out.

'Ayissa! Ayissa!' cried the widow. 'Oh, my little daughter, my little daughter, where are you?'

Then at last, from deep within the mound, a muffled voice answered, 'I'm . . . here.'

'Dig deeper, my dogs, dig deeper – tear the mound to pieces!' cried the widow.

The four great dogs set to with a will, working with teeth and paws, tossing aside the earth, dragging away the stones, till all lay scattered and tumbled about them. And where the mound had been there stood only the widow's great earthenware pot.

'Ayissa, Ayissa, little daughter, where are you?'

And from inside the pot came a stifled answer: 'I'm – here!'

Then the widow lifted the lid off the pot, and Ayissa scrambled out. And there she was, clasped in her mother's arms, with Shato, and Fari, and Samanduna and Samanbussa jumping round the two of them, wagging their tails and barking joyously.

So they all went home together. The widow gave Ayissa some hot milk and put her to bed. And from her market basket she took meat and oatmeal, and cooked the dogs the biggest and best supper they had ever eaten.

And after that they all lived happily, fearing nothing by day or by night, since Gogo would never come again to trouble them.

5 · Prince Lindworm

Once upon a time a king and queen were very sad, because they had no children. And early on a spring morning the queen went walking in the garden. The birds were singing, and rabbits were playing on the grass.

'Ah me,' thought the queen, 'in the birds' nests there are young ones, in the rabbit burrows there are babies, but in the palace there are none.'

And she wept.

Then there came to her a little old fairy woman, who said, 'Queen, dry your eyes. I know your sorrow, and I can help you. You wish for a son? Well, well, if you do as I tell you to do, you shall have not only one son, but two. Now listen carefully. When you go to bed tonight, have, set in your room, a bath filled with clear spring water. When you have taken your bath, you will find, lying beside it, two fruits. These you must peel and eat; and in the fullness of time you shall have twin babies. But remember to peel the fruits before you eat them, for that is important.'

Then the little old fairy vanished. And the queen went back into the palace, greatly comforted.

Well, that night the queen did as the fairy had told her. The bath was prepared, the queen bathed; and sure enough, when she stepped out of the bath, there, lying on the carpet, were two pearly-coloured fruits, of a kind she had never seen before.

The queen was so excited that she didn't even wait to dry herself: she quickly picked up one fruit and ate it. It tasted delicious, but – oh dear me! – in her haste she had forgotten to peel it. Well, there – what difference could it make? And she picked up the second fruit.

D

'But I will peel this one,' she told herself. And so she did, and found that the fruit had seven skins. All of these skins she peeled off before she ate the fruit. This second fruit tasted just as delicious as the first one. So she dried herself and went to bed warm and happy, and dreamed of the two little sons that the old fairy had promised her. The loveliest babies in the world they were that the queen dreamed of.

But alas, alas, when the months had passed and the queen gave birth, the first thing she brought into the world was a hideous Lindworm, which is a kind of serpent. But the queen had scarcely looked on it, before one of her waiting women snatched it up and flung it out of the window. . . . And the queen gave birth to her second baby: as lovely a little prince as ever the sun shone on.

Well, the Lindworm snaked away into the forest, and the queen tried to forget that it had ever been born. She swore her waiting women to secrecy, and they none of them said a word about it to anyone. The baby prince was shown to the king and to the whole court. The bells rang out, bonfires blazed, everyone rejoiced. . . .

So the years passed. Sometimes the queen thought she ought to tell the king about the Lindworm. But then again she thought, 'Why distress him?' So she did not tell him. And the baby prince grew into a handsome little boy, and then into a handsome big boy, and then into a young man, as good as he was handsome. The queen loved him, the king loved him, everybody loved him.

And one day the king said, 'Son, it is time you married. There are many beautiful princesses in the world, and there is not one but would be proud to be your wife. Ride out now into all the neighbouring kingdoms, and choose your bride.'

Then the prince put on his best clothes and set out in a golden coach drawn by six magnificent horses, with a coachman and postilion in scarlet livery, and a train of gaily dressed outriders trotting behind and before – all very grand, as befitted a gay young prince. But when they came to the first crossroads – what did they see? An enormous and hideous Lindworm lying right across the way, mouth open, fangs clashing, tail lashing.

And the Lindworm roared out, 'Where do you drive?'

'I drive to seek my bride,' said the prince. 'And I should be grateful if you would remove yourself from my road.'

But the Lindworm roared out, 'I am the first born! A bride for me before a bride for you!'

The prince told the coachman to drive on. But the Lindworm lashed with his spiked tail, and spat fire from his gaping jaws. The horses reared and plunged, swung round and screamed with fright. There was nothing for it but to drive back to the palace.

When the king heard about the Lindworm he said he would summon his army and march out to kill the beast. But the queen cried 'No, no, no!' And she wept, and fell on her knees, and told the king that the creature was his own son, the elder of the twins she had borne.

The king, who couldn't bear to see his queen in tears, didn't say, 'You should have told me this before,' which he very well might have done. He merely said that the prince should set out again next day, when perhaps the Lindworm would have gone back into the forest.

The prince did set out again next day, but the same thing happened. There was the Lindworm at the crossroads, straddled right across the way, lashing his spiked tail, spitting fire, and roaring out, 'I am the elder! I am the first born! A bride for me before a bride for you!'

Again the prince had to turn back. And again on the following day he set out, and the same thing happened. The Lindworm was waiting at the crossroads; the horses took fright, they reared, plunged, swung round. And there was the whole procession galloping in a disorderly rout back to the palace.

'This is truly outrageous!' said the king. 'In my own realm to be flouted by an unmannerly monster! And one that because he is my own son, I cannot take up arms against! We must try what reason will do. You shall set out again tomorrow, Prince, and speak the monster fair.'

So for the fourth time the prince set out. But there was no speaking the monster fair. Again he spat fire, again he lashed his spiked tail, and again he roared out, 'I am the first born! A bride for me before a bride for you!'

And for the fourth time the horses plunged and reared, again they screamed with fright; and the whole procession turned tail and galloped in confusion back to the palace.

'Very well,' said the king, 'we will invite the creature to the palace, and we will find him a bride.'

It was all very well for the king to say he would invite the Lindworm to the palace – but who was to carry the message? The king sent soldiers with a written invitation – but they fled at the sight of the monster. The king then sent an ambassador; but as soon as the ambassador approached the crossroads the Lindworm spat fire at him and bade him take himself off. The king sent his prime minister – the same thing happened. The king sent a company of handsome young pages, who went reluctantly, hand in hand, and trembling. But the Lindworm had them scampering back in a trice, with the message undelivered.

So in the end the prince himself went with the invitation, and then the Lindworm was satisfied and said, 'Yes, I will come.'

And come he did, to everyone's horror, though he behaved quietly enough.

Then the king sent his ambassador to the ruler of a small kingdom a long way off, asking for one of the ruler's daughters as a bride for his eldest son.

The ruler of the small far-off kingdom, who had never heard of the Lindworm, was flattered. He sent his eldest daughter. The poor girl arrived, but she was not introduced to her bridegroom until she stood before the altar. Then it was too late to turn back: the wedding was held, and though it was all very grand, the bride fainted with terror. In a faint she was carried up to the bridal chamber and left with the Lindworm, who promptly swallowed her, and spent the night sleeping off his heavy meal.

And in the morning he went back into the forest.

Surely now the king had done all that was required of him! And once more the prince set out to seek a bride for himself. But again there at the crossroads was the Lindworm, spitting fire and roaring,

'I am the first born! A bride for me before a bride for you!'

It was useless for the prince to point out that the Lindworm had already been given a bride. The monster merely gnashed his teeth and shouted that a girl who fainted at the sight of her bridegroom was no fit bride for anyone.

So again the prince had to turn back; and again the Lindworm was invited to the palace, and the king sent an embassy to another small distant country, asking for a princess as a bride for his eldest son. And again a princess arrived and was married and swallowed down. And again the Lindworm went back to the forest.

'Now surely the creature must be satisfied,' said the king. 'And you, my dear son, shall ride forth to seek *your* bride.'

But no, the Lindworm wasn't having that! There he was at the crossroads spitting fire and roaring out, 'I am the first born! A bride for me before a bride for you!'

And the prince had to turn back, and tell his father that he must find the Lindworm yet a third bride.

The king struck his hands together and cried out, 'I cannot do it! Already two kingdoms are threatening me with war!'

'Then I must fight the creature,' said the prince, 'even though he is my brother.'

But this the king would not allow. '*What* – and have you also swallowed up?' he cried. 'And leave the kingdom without an heir, and the queen and myself with broken hearts? No, no, no! I *will* find the creature a third bride! But not a princess, I will find him some poor girl who may be willing to sacrifice her life for the sake of enriching her family.'

And he flung off his crown, wrapped himself in a fur cloak, and hurried out of the palace.

Now not far from the king's city, in a tumbledown cottage, there lived a poor shepherd who had a young daughter, very good, very gentle, very pretty. And it was to this cottage that the king went hurrying. It was late afternoon, and the shepherd was bringing his flock in from the fields when the king met him.

Without wasting words, the king told the shepherd that he must send his daughter to the palace to be married to the Lindworm.

'And in return,' said the king, 'I will make you the richest man in my kingdom.'

But the shepherd shook his head. 'I would rather stay poor and keep my daughter,' he said. 'For I hear that the Lindworm has already swallowed down two wives.'

The king argued, the king pleaded, the shepherd said no, and no, and no. So at last the king lost his temper and said that being king he should and would be obeyed, and that if the shepherd didn't send his daughter to be married to the Lindworm, then the shepherd should lose his head. 'And your precious daughter shall lose hers too!' he shouted, in a most unkingly manner, and stamped back to the palace, feeling thoroughly desperate and ashamed of himself. But what else could he do?

The shepherd went home and told his daughter. Poor girl, how she wept! She ran out of the cottage and away into the forest, thinking to hide herself. She ran and ran till she had no strength to run farther. Then she sat down under an oak and sobbed.

And out from the oak stepped the old fairy who had given the queen the two fruits. And the old fairy said, 'Little daughter, why do you weep?'

'Oh, little mother, little mother, I have good cause to weep! The king has bidden me marry the Lindworm: the Lindworm who has already devoured two brides, and I shall be the third! I would do much for my dear father's sake, but this is too dreadful, too dreadful!'

But the old fairy said, 'Come, dry your eyes. If you will do exactly as I tell you, you shall not be eaten. You shall, on the other hand, deliver the kingdom from this evil, and be yourself a happy bride.'

And she told the girl exactly what she must do.

'It – it sounds rather terrible,' said the girl.

'It is either that or be eaten,' said the old fairy.

Then she went back into the oak, and the girl went home and told her father that she was ready to marry the Lindworm.

'No, no, no!' cried the shepherd. 'No! No! Rather than that I will leave my flock and we will run away! We will go hand in hand into another kingdom, and there beg our bread!'

But the girl said, 'Don't fret, little father, for I believe that all will be well. In the forest I met an old fairy. And the fairy told me what I must do to save both myself and this unhappy country.'

Then she kissed her father, and went to the palace to tell the king that she was willing to marry the Lindworm.

The king was overjoyed. He sent the shepherd a sackful of gold, and ordered a magnificent wedding dress to be made for the girl. Very beautiful she looked when she stood before the altar; and more hideous than hideous, and more terrible than terrible, looked the Lindworm who stood by her side. The priest who married them stammered and stuttered and hurried over the marriage service, and the hair rose on his scalp with the horror and the pity of it. But the words were spoken, the girl and the Lindworm were married, and the wedding feast was held. The Lindworm golloped down everything that was set before him with relish, though nobody else could swallow more than a mouthful.

Now you must know that before the wedding, the girl had put on seven white shifts under her bridal dress, and she had asked that a bath full of warm soapy water, and another bath tub full of fresh milk, together with a goodly supply of new scrubbing brushes, should be put in the bridal chamber. And though it seemed a strange request, the king had said, 'Yes, yes, let her have anything she asks for, poor girl, anything at all!'

So, after the wedding feast, when the lovely bride and the hideous bridegroom were conducted by a goodly company of lords and ladies to the sound of music and the blazing of torches to the bridal chamber, there, set on the floor beside the bed, were the two bath tubs, one full of soapy water, and the other full of fresh milk, together with a little pile of new scrubbing brushes.

Now the dreadful moment had come: the torches were put out, the music ceased, the door of the bridal chamber was shut on the girl and the Lindworm, and the procession of lords and ladies went back to the banqueting hall.

'Oh, poor girl, poor pretty girl!' The ladies were weeping, the lords walked with downcast eyes.

And in the bridal chamber, the Lindworm glared at his bride and roared out, 'Maiden, shed a shift!'

'Prince Lindworm,' answered the girl, 'shed a skin.'

'No one has dared to tell me to do that before!' roared the Lindworm.

'But I am telling you now,' said the girl.

The Lindworm opened his great jaws, out darted his forked tongue, his mouthful of great teeth snapped gleaming in the lamplight. Was he going to swallow her down? No. Writhing and groaning, groaning and writhing, he cast his outer skin. There it lay on the floor.

And the girl drew off her bridal dress and one of her seven shifts, and laid them on top of the skin.

Again the Lindworm roared, 'Maiden, shed another shift!'

And the girl answered, 'Prince Lindworm, shed another skin.'

'Do you dare to tell me to do that a second time?' roared the Lindworm.

'Yes, I dare,' answered the girl.

So, groaning and writhing, moaning and muttering, the Lindworm cast another skin. There it lay on the floor. And the girl took off her second shift and laid it on top of the skin.

And for the third time the Lindworm roared, 'Maiden, shed another shift!'

And for the third time the girl answered, 'Prince Lindworm, shed another skin!'

'No one has dared to tell me to do that a third time!' roared the Lindworm.

'But I am telling you now,' said the girl.

And moaning and groaning, writhing and muttering, the Lindworm struggled out of his third skin. There it lay on top of the others. And the girl took off her third shift and put it on top of the skin.

So it went on. Again the Lindworm ordered the girl to shed a shift, again she bade him shed a skin, and willy nilly it seemed he must do as she bade him, until there on the floor lay his seven skins, and on them lay six of the girl's shifts; but the seventh she need not

take off, because the Lindworm was now stretched on the floor, a shapeless mass of flesh, with no skin on him at all.

Then the girl snatched up one of the scrubbing brushes, dipped it in the warm soapy water, and began to scrub away at that shapeless mass with all her strength. She scrubbed, scrubbed, scrubbed; and as she scrubbed, the shapeless mass began to take form again, but not its old form. It was taking the form of a man, it was taking the form of a prince, a prince who became more and more beautiful to look on with every scrub she gave him. And when the scrubbing brushes were all worn out, the girl dipped a sponge into the tub of fresh milk, and gently washed the prince from head to feet. And he stood up smiling, and dried himself, and took the girl in his arms.

'Oh, my dear brave girl,' cried the handsome prince. 'Oh, my dear brave girl! How can I ever repay you for what you have done for me?'

'Just by loving me,' said the happy girl. . . .

The king had not slept well that night. Early in the morning he sent a page to the bridal chamber to see what had happened there. The page went unwillingly – it was not an errand he took any pleasure in, you may be sure. Fearfully he tapped at the door of the bridal chamber, but got no answer. He hoped that the door might be locked, but it was not. Fearfully he pushed it open, and slipped into the room. What did he see? In a heap on the floor seven scaly skins, a bridal dress and six white shifts, and in the bed the shepherd's daughter, asleep in the arms of a handsome prince.

The page ran to tell the king. King and queen hurried to the bridal chamber. The sleeping prince woke and sat up, huddling the blankets round him.

'Dear Father,' he said, 'if I might crave a robe to cover my nakedness?'

'A robe!' shouted the king. 'You may crave a kingdom!'

And he burst into happy tears.

The news spread like wildfire through the palace, and through the city, and through all the country round. Everyone went wild with joy. The shepherd came hurrying to the palace to clasp his daughter in his arms. The younger twin prince set off once more in his gilded coach to seek a bride. This time he met no monster at the crossroads, and soon returned with a pretty young princess. Now there was another wedding. And if the former wedding had been a sad affair, this second wedding was joyous indeed.

So the bells rang out, the bonfires blazed, all the people cried 'Hurrah!' And the king, the queen, the two princes and their beautiful brides lived in happiness ever after.

6 · The Monster in the Mill

Once upon a time there was a good little maiden whose mother had died. And what did her silly father do but marry a shrew of a woman who hated our good little maiden.

Now the maiden's father was a farmer, and he also owned a mill; but the mill was no use to him, or to any man, because there was a monster who came into the mill every night and ate up anyone he found there. And of course the stepmother got to know about the monster, and she said to herself, 'Ah ha! Ah ha!' Then she called our good little maiden, gave her some bread in a basket, and said, 'Dear child, I want you tonight to go down to the mill and keep guard there. Here's the key. Lock the door and bolt the window, and see that no one comes in.'

Well, this maiden was an obedient little maiden, she always did what she was told. And after she had set ready her stepmother's tea, and prepared everything for her father's supper when he came in from the fields, she took the basket full of bread, and also a fishing rod, and went down to the mill.

Why did she take a fishing rod? Well to be sure, it was to catch some fish in the mill race for her own supper, because dry bread isn't very appetizing. So she came into the valley where the mill was, and sat down on a bit of a rock by the mill race, unwound the line from her fishing rod, cast in the line, and caught four fish.

Then she unlocked the mill house door, and went in.

What did she see inside? She saw a bright fire burning, and sitting before the fire she saw little Cat and little Dog and little Cock. Little Cat and little Dog and little Cock were very pleased to see the maiden: they welcomed her with purrs and barks and cluck-cluck-cluckings. And they were more pleased still when she fried the fish and opened her basket and divided her supper into four equal shares, one share for each of them.

But, before this, she had locked the door and bolted the window, so that no one from outside could come in.

When the maiden and little Cat and little Dog and little Cock had all eaten their fill, they settled themselves down comfortably before the fire. The maiden was drowsy, but little Dog said, 'Is the door fast locked, is the window fast barred?'

'Yes,' said the maiden. And she yawned.

Then little Dog said, 'Keep awake! Keep awake! You mustn't fall asleep before the cock crows! And if someone comes knocking at the door, don't let them in before you have asked one of us.'

'All right,' said the maiden. And she yawned again. She would have fallen asleep, only little Dog kept nudging her, and little Cat kept slapping her with his paw, and little Cock kept tweaking her hair.

And by and by someone did knock at the door, and a gruff voice cried, '*Hupp! Hupp! Hupp!* Little maiden, let me in!'

Then the maiden whispered to little Dog, 'Who is that, out there?'

And little Dog answered, 'That out there is the Mill Monster.'

So the maiden whispered to little Cat, 'Then what shall we do?'

And little Cat answered, 'Tell him you won't open the door until he has brought you all the money that he has stolen and keeps hidden in his cave.'

So the maiden called out loud and clear, 'Yes, I will open the door; but first you must bring me all the money you keep hidden in your cave.'

The monster went away then. By and by he came back. He was carrying a huge sack full of money.

'*Hupp! Hupp! Hupp!* Little maiden, I've brought the money. Open the door and let me in!'

Then the maiden whispered to little Dog, 'What am I to do now?'

'Tell him to make a hole in the thatch and throw the money down,' said little Dog.

61

So the maiden did that; and the monster climbed on to the roof. He tore a hole in the thatch with his claws, and emptied the sack full of gold down into the hole: *Clitter-clatter, chinkle-chinkle, chink!* Down tumbled the gold on to the floor. And the monster put one great rolling eye to the hole and called out, 'I see you! I see you! Now open the door, I want my supper!'

'Oh, little Cock,' whispered the maiden, 'what shall we do now?'

And little Cock answered, 'Now it is time for cocks to crow, for dawn is in the sky!'

And he planted his feet firmly, threw back his head, opened his beak wide, and cried out, '*Erk-er-oodle-o-o-o!*'

'*Wow-wow-wow*, the Sun is rising!' shouted little Dog.

'*Mi-ow-ow-ow!* The Sun! The Sun!' cried little Cat.

And the monster flung down the empty sack and fled away.

Then the maiden filled her basket with gold coins and went home. She gave the gold to her stepmother and said, 'There's a lot more down on the mill floor.'

'*More!*' shouted the stepmother. '*More*, did you say?'

And she snatched up bags and baskets, rushed down to the mill, and spent all day gathering up the gold from the floor.

In the evening she gave the little maiden a basket full of bread, and sent her down to the mill again. She was hoping the monster would eat the little maiden; she was also hoping that the monster would give the little maiden more gold. She didn't know which she would like best – to get rid of the maiden, or to get some more gold.

Well, this night as last night, little Cat and little Dog and little Cock were sitting by the fire inside the mill. The maiden caught some fish, went into the mill, locked the door and bolted the window, fried the fish, opened her basket, and divided her supper into four equal shares. And they had only just finished supper, when it was *bang, bang, bang* and *rattle, rattle, rattle* at the door, and the monster shouting '*Hupp! Hupp! Hupp!* Little maiden, let me come in!'

And the maiden whispered, 'Oh, little Cat, what shall we do?'

Little Cat answered, 'Tell him you won't open the door until he has brought you all the other stolen treasures he keeps in his cave.'

So then the maiden called out loud and clear, 'Yes, I will open the door; but first you must bring me all the other stolen treasures you keep in your cave.'

The monster went away then. He was gone a long time. When he came back it was *bump, bump, bump,* and *clatter, clatter, clatter,* and the monster panting and groaning and stumbling under the weight of his treasures.

'*Hupp! Hupp! Hupp!* Little maiden, here's everything I possess! *Now* open the door!'

And the maiden whispered 'Oh, little Dog, what am I to do now?'

'Tell him to break the window and throw in the treasures,' said little Dog.

So the maiden did that, and the monster struck the window glass with his great fist and broke it. Then he began tossing in his treasures. There were beautiful clothes, and bales of velvet and silk, and wonderful tapestries, and silver dishes, and gold candlesticks and furnishings the like of which you might never hope to see outside a king's palace. The monster was tossing all these things in as fast as snow falling, the pile inside the mill was growing bigger and bigger, and the pile outside the mill was growing less and less, until there was only one thing left to get in through the window, and that was a big handsome chest, ornamented with painted scrolls and jewelled flowers. The monster had the chest against the window, and was pushing and panting to get it through, and calling out, 'This is the end! This is all! Now, little maiden, open the door!'

'Oh, little Cock,' whispered the maiden, 'what to do now?'

And little Cock answered, 'Now it is time for cocks to crow, for dawn is in the sky.'

Then he planted his feet firmly, threw back his head, opened his beak wide, and cried out, '*Erk-er-oodle o-o-o!*'

Little Dog barked, little Cat mewed, the little maiden clapped her hands, a ray of sunlight wavered through the broken window, the monster dropped the big handsome chest, and fled howling.

My word, what fun the little maiden and Cock and Dog and Cat had after that – rummaging through all the beautiful things and dressing themselves up! Cock stuck a diamond in his crest, Dog found a collar beaded with rubies, Cat put on a green velvet cloak, and marched about fanning herself with a lace fan ornamented with softly glimmering pearls. As for the little maiden, she was trying on one beautiful dress after another, and calling out, 'Does this one suit me best, or does this other one suit me better?'

'You look lovely in all of them,' they told her.

And truly she did.

So the morning wore on, and back at the farm the stepmother was grinning and saying to herself, 'My fine maiden hasn't come home! My fine maiden isn't coming home any more! Yes, this time the monster has gobbled her up!'

Then she took a sack and strode down to the mill, to see if the monster had left any more gold on the floor.

When they heard the *clump*, *clump* of the stepmother's footsteps, little Cat and little Dog and little Cock ran to hide themselves; and there was the little maiden, dressed in a shimmering robe, standing all alone among the heaped up treasures.

Shouting with rage and astonishment the stepmother snatched the robe off her, boxed her ears, seized her by the arm, and hustled her home. Then she ordered out horses and carts, and summoned labourers, and went back with them to the mill to bring home the treasures. All the afternoon the men worked hard, dragging the treasures out of the mill in cartload after cartload, and driving the full carts up to the farmhouse. By the time they had finished, the farmhouse was stacked with treasures – enough you'd think to satisfy anyone.

But no, the stepmother wasn't satisfied. She was thinking, 'If the monster has any more treasures I'm going to have them! Tonight I shall keep watch myself.'

So at twilight she took a hamper full of food and a bottle of wine and stamped off down to the mill.

Little Cat and little Dog and little Cock were sitting in front of the fire. 'What do you think *you're* doing here, you wretched creatures?' cried the stepmother. And she smacked little Cat, and kicked little Dog, and threw a stool at little Cock.

'*Me-ow! Wow, wow, wow! Kek, kek, kek!*' they cried and ran out. The stepmother laughed, locked the door, and sat down to eat her supper. And she had only just finished eating when there came a bang at the door, and the monster calling, '*Hupp! Hupp! Hupp!* Old lady, let me in!'

'Oh, certainly, sir! You are more than welcome, sir!' cried the stepmother. And she minced to the door and flung it wide.

What happened? The monster gave a kick and a jump, he opened his great jaws, *gulp, gulp*, he swallowed down the stepmother, head first. Then he yawned, smacked his lips, lay by the fire, and slept. . . .

And by and by little Cock and little Dog and little Cat came to stand outside the broken window.

'*Erk-er-doodle do-o-o!*' cried little Cock. 'Dawn is in the sky!'

'*Bow-wow-wow!* The Sun is rising!' cried little Dog.

'*Me-ow-ow-ow!* The Sun! The Sun!' cried little Cat.

Inside the mill the monster woke up, strode out through the open door, and went back to his cave. He was muttering and grumbling;

his stepmother-supper had disagreed with him – he had a pain in his stomach and a bitter taste in his mouth.

Back at the farm the little maiden was busy cooking her father's breakfast when little Cock and little Cat and little Dog came running in. 'She's gone!' cried little Cock. 'The stepmother's gone!' cried little Dog. 'And we don't think she's ever coming back!' cried little Cat. 'Hurrah! Hurrah! Hurrah!' they shouted, and danced round the little maiden.

Well, of course the stepmother didn't come back. And the monster didn't come back either, because the farmer burned down the mill. He didn't ask what had become of the stepmother: truth to tell he was glad to be rid of her, and he was in a very good temper. So when the little maiden asked if Dog and Cat and Cock might come to live with her at the farm, he said, 'Why yes, if it pleases you.'

So after that they all lived merrily.

7 · Dunber

Once upon a time there was a monster called Dunber, and he built himself a house on the top of a mountain. Monster **Dunber** had claws on his hands and claws on his feet; he had a bear's head and a great hairy body, and three men standing on each other's shoulders wouldn't have reached higher than his waist. He didn't often come down from his mountain, and that was a mercy. But in stormy weather you could hear his voice carried on the wind, and roaring out a song:

> '*Hey, hey, Dunberonday,*
> *What shall he have for his dinner today?*
> *If a traveller or two should come this way*
> *They'd get a kind welcome from Dunberonday!*
> *Hey, hey, Dunberonday,*
> *He's a fine old fellow is Dunberonday!*'

Well of course travellers didn't go that way. They said a prayer and hurried past the foot of the mountain faster than fast!

At the foot of the mountain was a little wood and beyond the wood a field or two; and beyond the wood and the fields lived a peasant called Kurt. Kurt's wife had died a long time ago, but he had two pretty daughters, called Wanda and Clare.

Now one day in late autumn Kurt went into the wood to collect logs for the fire. It was very cold, and under the trees the ground was already frozen. And as Kurt was returning home with a great load of logs, he slipped on some ice and twisted his ankle. My word, that hurt! He hobbled home as best he could, and when he went in – what did he find? The girls away at market, the kitchen fire gone out, and no means of rekindling it.

Kurt limped to the door, looked about him, and saw up there on the top of the mountain a bright flicker of flames. Yes, Monster Dunber had a fire all right – plague take him!

'If it wasn't for this ankle of mine, I'd risk going up to borrow a burning brand,' thought Kurt. 'But short of crawling on hands and knees, I don't see how it can be done.'

So, when the girls came home from market with their laden baskets, he said to Wanda, 'Little daughter, go up there – up there on the mountain where a fire is burning, and ask for the loan of a lighted brand.'

'But, Father,' said Wanda, 'don't you know who lives up there?'

'I know well enough,' said Kurt. 'But if you curtsey your best and speak your prettiest, I don't think Dunber will have the heart to hurt you. And without fire we shall soon all three die of cold.'

So Wanda put down her basket and set out. She had a stiff climb of it, and when she came to Dunber's house, she found him sitting by the fire, cracking nuts.

'Hey, hey, pretty little may,
And what has brought you up this way?'

roared Dunber.

Wanda curtseyed to the ground and said, 'Oh, if you please, kind sir, we are poor peasants who live at the bottom of your mountain. My father has slipped on the ice and sprained his ankle, and our fire has gone out. So, if you please, kind sir, I have come to borrow a lighted brand.'

Dunber was in a good temper. He had just had his dinner, and he was feeling full and satisfied. So he said, 'Well, all right, you shall have a brand, but first you must comb my hair for an hour. Can you sing? And do you know any good tunes?'

'Yes, I can sing,' said Wanda. 'And I know a tune or two.'

'Then comb and sing, comb and sing,' said Dunber. And he gave Wanda a huge comb with teeth like a rake. Then he lay down with his great head on a cushion. And Wanda began to comb his bristly hair. And as she combed she sang.

68

Dunber yawned and shut his eyes. 'That's a pretty tune,' he mumbled. 'Now – sing me – 'nother.'

So Wanda sang another song, and yet another. And Dunber muttered and grinned and yawned: in half an hour he was fast asleep. He was wearing a gold chain round his neck, and the firelight gleamed on the gold.

Wanda couldn't keep her eyes off that chain. A hairy old monster wearing such a beautiful thing – it was absurd! How much better it would look round *her* white neck! She wanted that chain, she wanted it – she must have it! Very softly Wanda undid the clasp, slipped the chain from Dunber's neck, and fastened it, in many loops, round her own neck. Then she took a burning brand from the fire, and ran out of the house. She ran down the mountain and into the wood.

In the middle of the wood she saw a plum tree, where never a plum tree had been before. The branches of the tree were drooping almost to the ground with ripe, rosy fruit, and it called out, 'Little maiden, shake me, shake me, lest all my branches break!'

But Wanda answered, 'I have no time to stop!' And she ran on.

Very soon she came to a pear tree, where never a pear tree had stood before. The branches of the tree were bowed down to the ground with big ripe pears, and it called out, 'Little maiden, little maiden, shake me, shake me, lest all my branches break!'

But Wanda answered, 'I have no time!' And she ran on, and came to the edge of the wood. And there she saw a baker's oven, where never an oven had been before. The oven was full of cakes and it called out, 'Little maiden, take out the cakes or they will burn!'

But Wanda answered, 'I have no time!' And she raced on. . . .

Up on the top of the mountain Monster Dunber woke. He yawned, rubbed his claws across his eyes, felt for the chain round his neck. What! The chain not there, and the maiden not there! 'Thief! Thief!' Dunber roared, ran out of his house, and bounded down the mountain after Wanda.

He came into the wood; he came to the plum tree.

'Plum tree, plum tree, have you seen a maiden running, with a brand burning, and a golden chain about her neck?'

'Yes,' said the plum tree. 'She went that way.'

Dunber raced on. He was running, running. Wanda was running, running. Dunber came to the pear tree.

'Pear tree, pear tree, have you seen a maiden running, with a brand burning, and a golden chain about her neck?'

'Yes,' said the pear tree. 'She went that way.'

Dunber raced on. He was running, running. Wanda was running, running. Dunber came to the bake oven.

'Bake oven, bake oven, have you seen a maiden running, with a brand burning, and a golden chain about her neck?'

'Yes,' said the oven. 'She went that way. *And there she is!*'

Yes, there was Wanda, running, running, but now not many paces ahead. Dunber roared, Wanda screamed, snatched the golden chain from her neck, and threw it down. Dunber gave a bound, picked up the chain, gave another bound, stretched out a long arm, caught up Wanda, carried her back to his house on the mountain, and shut her up in a box. Then he put the gold chain round his neck, sat down before the fire, and roared out a song:

> *'Hey, hey, Dunberonday!*
> *Dunber has caught a naughty little may,*
> *And in his box she shall safely stay,*
> *For Dunber has had his dinner today,*
> *But tomorrow is another day,*
> *And Dunber will roast the naughty little may,*
> *Hey, hey, Dunberonday!'*

And back in the cottage at the bottom of the mountain Kurt said to Clare, 'Your sister is a long time coming with that brand. She has surely met with some misfortune! Fire we must have, or we shall freeze to death this winter. That old Dunber has fire. Go up the mountain and borrow a brand.'

So Clare went up the mountain, and everything happened as before. She found Dunber sitting by the fire, she asked for a brand. Dunber said she should have it, but first she must comb his hair for an hour and sing to him.

Well, she did that, and in half an hour Dunber was sound asleep.

Then there came a whispering and a whimpering out of a big box that stood in a corner of the room, 'Sister, sister, let me out!'

Clare lifted the lid of the box, and out scrambled Wanda. Wanda wanted to take the gold chain from Dunber's neck; but Clare whispered, 'No, no, we are not thieves! We will only take the brand that Dunber promised me.' So she took a burning brand from the fire, and she and Wanda tiptoed out of the room, and ran down the mountain.

They came into the wood, and there was the plum tree laden down with fruit. And the plum tree called out, 'Little maidens, shake me, shake me, lest all my branches break!'

'No!' cried Wanda. 'We haven't time!'

And she ran on.

But Clare said, 'We haven't much time, poor tree; but to shake you won't take long.'

And she took hold of one branch after another, and shook and shook, till all the plums lay scattered on the ground. Then she ran on after Wanda, and the plum tree called out, 'Thank you, little maiden! You have helped me, and when I can I will help you.'

Clare ran, Wanda ran: they came to the pear tree. The branches of the pear tree were bowed to the ground with big ripe pears. And the tree called out, 'Little maidens, shake me, shake me, lest all my branches break!'

'No, no, *no!*' shrieked Wanda, racing past the tree. 'We haven't time!'

But Clare said, 'Oh yes, poor tree, I think we have time for that.'

And she took hold of the branches and shook, shook, till all the pears lay on the ground. And the tree lifted up its branches and said, 'Thank you, little maiden! You have helped me, and when I can I will help you.'

Clare ran on after Wanda. They came to the edge of the wood, and there stood the baker's oven. And the oven called out, 'My cakes will burn, my cakes will burn – little maidens, take them out!'

'No, no!' shrieked Wanda. 'We haven't time!'

And she ran on.

But Clare said, 'We must make time for that!' And she opened the

71

oven door, took out the cakes, laid them on the ground, and ran on.
And the oven called after her, 'Thank you, little maiden! You have
helped me, and when I can I will help you!'

But up on the mountain Dunber waked from sleep. He rubbed his
claws across his eyes, stared about him. *What!* The box empty, both
maidens gone! He roared in his rage and set off down the mountain.

In the wood he came to the plum tree.

'Plum tree, plum tree, have you seen two maidens running, and a
brand burning?'

'No,' said the plum tree. 'I have seen nothing.'

'Then who shook down your plums?' roared Dunber.

'Oh, the wind did that,' said the plum tree.

'You lie!' roared Dunber. And he gave the plum tree a kick that
tore it up by the roots and sent it flying. Then he gobbled up all the
plums that lay on the ground, raced on, and came to the pear tree.

'Pear tree, pear tree, have you seen two maidens running, and a
brand burning?'

'Oh no,' said the pear tree, 'I have seen nothing like that!'

'Then who shook down your pears, who shook them down?'

'Oh,' said the pear tree, 'I shook them down myself.'

'You lie!' roared Dunber. And he gave the pear tree a kick that tore it up by the roots and sent it flying. Then he gobbled up all the pears that lay on the ground, ran on, and came to the oven.

'Oven, oven, have you seen two maidens running, and a brand burning?'

'Certainly not!' said the oven.

'Then who took out your cakes, who did that?' roared Dunber.

'Oh,' said the oven, 'a little elf did that.'

'You lie!' shouted Dunber. And he gave the oven a kick that sent it rolling over and over. Then he gobbled up all the cakes that lay on the ground, and smacked his lips.

Now he felt full and lazy. Why run any farther? After all the maidens had only taken a burning brand, and that he had promised them. He patted the gold chain round his neck, and thought of Clare.

'That was a good little maid,' said he. '*She* wouldn't steal a body's golden chain. And the other one – bah! She's not worth bothering about!'

And he turned and stamped back up the mountain.

So Wanda and Clare came safely home with the burning brand. Their father stood at the door, looking out. And what did they see coming along behind them? What but the plum tree, and the pear tree, and the baker's oven!

'Plant us in your garden, little Clare, and we will give you fruit twice a day!' cried the plum tree and the pear tree.

And 'Take me in and set me up in the kitchen, little Clare,' cried the oven, 'and I will give you all the food you need!'

So Clare did that. She carried the oven into the kitchen. She planted the trees in the garden. She shook those trees twice every day, and all the year round they dropped down ripe, juicy plums and pears. As for the oven, whenever food was needed, Clare had only to open the oven door, and there was a meal all nicely cooked. So she and her father and Wanda lived now without a care.

They never went up the mountain again, nor did Dunber ever

come down to trouble them. He stroked the gold chain round his neck, poked his fire till it blazed, and sat watching the flames and singing:

'*Hey, hey, Dunberonday,*
Up on his mountain let him stay,
And the folk in the valley safe shall be,
As long as they don't come worriting me.
Ha, ha, ha, and hey, hey, hey,
What a good old fellow is Dunberonday!'

8 · The Story of the Three Young Shepherds

There was a peasant who owned a great flock of sheep. And when this peasant grew old and ill, and knew that he must soon die, he called his three sons to his bedside, and said, 'Sons, go into the forest, gather a big bundle of sticks, bind the bundle together with a strong rope, and bring it to me.'

Well, the sons did that: they gathered the sticks, bound them together with rope, and brought the bundle to their father.

'Now,' said the old peasant, 'break these sticks into fragments.'

'But, Father,' said the eldest son, 'in order to do that, we must first undo the rope that binds the sticks together.'

The peasant answered, 'My son, you speak truly. And as it is with this bundle of sticks, so it shall be with you three lads. Together no man shall break you; but apart you are but brittle. Promise me now that when I am gone you will stay together, and never divide the flock of sheep.'

So the sons promised; and the old peasant died in peace.

Well, the lads kept their promise. Every morning, after they had milked the ewes, one lad drove the great flock of sheep to pasture on the grassy hills that surrounded their cottage, whilst the other two stayed at home, and saw to the making of butter and cheese. And these duties they took in turns. But when shearing time came, they all three worked together. When the shearing was done, two of them set off for market, drawing the piled up wool in a handcart, and sold the wool for a good price. But, remembering their father's custom, they never slaughtered or sold either sheep or lamb. And

75

their flock grew ever greater: and the three lads lived for a year or two in perfect harmony and happiness.

But then came a time of drought: month after month no rain fell, the grass on the hills wilted and turned brown, the sheep were half famished, and grew so thin and weak that they could scarce walk.

'Oh me, our poor sheep – what can we do?' cried the eldest lad, Konrad. And the second lad, Fabian, wiped the tears from his eyes and said, 'It seems we can do nothing but watch them die!'

But the youngest lad, Karl, said, 'No, no! We must not let them die! Let us seek new pastures on the other side of the great forest. I have heard that a river flows there, and where there is a river, the grass may yet be green. Come, let us set out at once, and drive the flock there, whilst yet the poor beasts can stand on their legs!'

So that's what they did. They packed a few needful utensils – buckets, pannikins, shears, churn, and such like – into the handcart, locked up their cottage, and set off through the forest, driving their flock before them. For seven whole weeks they were driving their feeble flock through that great forest, but at last they came to the end of it. And where did they find themselves? In a broad fertile valley, where grass grew green and flowers grew bright, and a river flowed placidly among sheltering willows.

'Ah, why did we not come here before!' cried Konrad.

Then two of them set to work cutting down the willows and making a cabin, whilst the third watched over the flock, milked the ewes, and made the cheese and butter. And it wasn't long before the sheep grew fat and strong again; and it seemed to the three lads that they had discovered a little paradise, inhabited only by their three selves.

But at the head of the valley was a great stone castle; though from where the lads kept their flocks, this castle was hidden by the windings of the valley, and nothing of it could be seen but the tops of one or two huge stone chimneys standing up among the trees – chimneys that the lads took to be great grey rocks. For what with flock-tending and cabin-building they were yet too busy to explore that end of the valley.

But in the castle lived a monster called Jabor, who considered himself lord over the whole district. And one morning Jabor, thrusting his great head above the trees, thought he saw some tiny creatures moving about over the grass at the farther end of the valley.

Well, at first Jabor didn't trouble his dull wits to think what those tiny creatures might be; but when he had seen them again next morning, and again the morning after, he became curious. And that morning, Konrad, as he sat contentedly on the river bank, with the sheep grazing round him, was horrified to see what appeared to be a great mountain charging down upon him – and more horrified when he heard an enormous voice that roared out, '*Ha!* You miserable midget, what are you doing in my valley?'

Konrad fell on his knees. 'Oh my gracious lord, we are three brothers who came here from behind the great forest, from a parched country where our sheep were perishing. We didn't know that this land belonged to anyone!'

'Ha! So! Three brothers! What? Didn't know, eh? Well, I will let it pass. Hum! Ha! We will strike up a friendship, and I will help myself to seven of your sheep!'

So saying, Jabor scooped up seven of the fattest ewes and stuffed them into his pocket. Then he roared out, 'Hum! Ha! What's your name?'

'K-Konrad, my lord.'

'And I am Monster Jabor, a lord as you say – lord of the universe! You see that stone castle up there at the head of the valley? What – what? Can't see it? Eh? No matter, it's there, and it's where I live. Hum! I invite you to breakfast with me tomorrow. Ha! Bring seven more sheep. What, what, you make butter and cheese, do you? Bring seven cheeses then, and as much butter as you can carry. What, two brothers you say you have – and do you love your brothers? Hum! Ha! What's to prevent my swallowing them down, and you on top of them? Hey? Only my kind heart! Ha! Ha! What! Up *you* come to breakfast, or down *I* come and make a breakfast of the three of you. Ha! Ha! Ha!'

And off strode Monster Jabor, making the valley clang with his shouts of laughter.

Konrad hurriedly collected his flock together and drove them home. 'Brothers, brothers!' he cried. 'We must hasten to leave this valley!'

And he told them what had happened.

'But where are we to go?' said Fabian. 'We cannot run away and leave the flock behind us. And to pack up and drive them off will be a slow and lengthy business. And what is to prevent the monster from coming after us, and devouring the flock and us into the bargain? I think we must sacrifice seven more sheep, brother Konrad; and I think they must be driven up to this Monster Jabor's castle, first thing tomorrow morning. But I'll willingly go instead of you.'

'No, I am the youngest and least wanted,' said Karl. 'Let *me* go!'

'You shall neither of you go,' said Konrad. 'If one must go, it shall be myself.'

So next morning, very early, Konrad took seven cheeses and a pail full of butter, and set out for Monster Jabor's castle, driving seven sheep before him.

In the castle courtyard a fire was smouldering, and over the fire a huge cauldron, filled with porridge, hung on a crook. Jabor was still asleep, and the castle echoed with his snores. Konrad left the sheep in the courtyard, and carried the butter and the cheeses up into the bedroom, guided by Jabor's snores. He stood by the bed, shaking with fear, and not knowing what to do next. But suddenly Jabor opened his eyes.

'Ha! So you've come! What? Here's the butter I see, and here are the cheeses. Hum! Ha! Where are the sheep?'

'In the courtyard,' faltered Konrad.

'Ha! Ha! What? What? Afraid of me?' roared Jabor. 'So you should be – what?' And he seized the pailful of butter and swallowed it down, pail and all. Then he crammed the seven cheeses into his mouth, and bellowed, 'Where are the sheep, did you say?'

'In – in the courtyard, my lord.'

'Go and shut them up in the stable – you'll find the other seven there. Ha! I didn't eat a single sheep yesterday, and I'm not eating one today. Seven of my friends are coming on a visit the day after tomorrow, and we shall have a feast. Sheep in plenty, eh? And maybe some other juicy little fellows! What? What? Did you see a fire in a corner of the courtyard with a cauldron hanging over it?'

'Yes, my lord.'

'It's my breakfast porridge cooking. Go and stir it. If you let it burn – ha! ha! *you'll* burn with it! Do you want to go and burn in the cauldron? What? What?'

'N-no, my lord.'

'Well, be off and stir, be off and stir!' roared Jabor.

So, for half an hour or so, Konrad stood in the courtyard, stirring the porridge with a long iron spoon. 'Perhaps it's not going to be so bad, after all,' he thought. 'Perhaps Jabor will let me go home when I've finished stirring.'

But there he was mistaken. When Jabor came out, wiping his mouth with his fist, he seized up Konrad by the heels and flung him into the stable on top of the sheep. 'Ha! Ha!' he roared. 'So you haven't burned my porridge! What? What? Today you live, tomorrow you live, and *the day after tomorrow* we feast, my friends and I. We feast on sheep and little mannikins, sweet, tender little mannikins, whose bones go *crick, crack, crackle* in a monster's mouth!'

Then, having bolted the stable door, Jabor took the cauldron off the crook, swallowed the porridge at one gulp, smacked his lips, and strode off down into the valley, where he found Fabian tending the sheep.

'Ha! Ha!' roared Jabor. 'I had a good breakfast this morning! And your brother is staying with me for the present. A nice tender little boy is your brother. What? What? But if you graze your sheep in my valley, you must pay rent – that's only fair! What? So tomorrow, my chick, I invite *you* to breakfast. Hum! Ha! Bring seven more sheep, and seven more cheeses, and as much butter as you can carry. What? What? Do you hear me, hey? Mind you come! If you don't come, it will be the worse for you! See my finger, see my thumb? They can pinch, little chicken, they can pinch! Ha! Ha! Ha!'

Then Jabor, having picked up seven more sheep and stuffed them into his pocket, strode off back to his castle, and put those seven sheep also into his stable. He brought fodder for the sheep, and food and wine for Konrad. 'Eat up, eat up!' he roared. 'Ha! Ha! Can't have you pining away. What? What?'

The sheep were glad of the fodder, but Konrad, though he drank the wine, had no heart to eat.

Down in the valley Fabian and Karl spent an unhappy day; and early next morning, Fabian took seven cheeses and a pailful of butter and prepared to set out for the castle, with seven more sheep. 'Goodbye, my brother,' he said to Karl, 'may the Lord keep you! For I have a strong feeling that I shall never see you again.'

And Karl answered, 'But I have a stronger feeling that you *will* see me again! If we have to die, we will die together, as brothers should. And if we are to live, we will live and rejoice together. So keep up your heart, my brother.'

Well, exactly the same thing happened to Fabian as had happened to Konrad. He found Jabor in bed, gave him the butter and the cheeses, and was sent out into the courtyard to stir the porridge. And when the porridge was cooked, he was shut in the stable, along with Konrad and the sheep.

And again Jabor brought fodder for the sheep and food and wine for the two lads. 'No need to starve today, my chickens,' he roared. 'You don't go into the pot until tomorrow!'

Then he strode off down into the valley, where he found young Karl tending the sheep.

'Ah, good morning, good morning!' said Karl. 'I was expecting you. How are my brothers?'

'Eating hearty and doing well,' roared Jabor. 'And hoping you will join them for breakfast tomorrow morning. Hey? What?'

'I shall be happy to do so,' said Karl. 'But keep your distance, if you please; for your breath is so powerful that I find it difficult to stand on my feet.'

Monster Jabor stared; he didn't quite know what to make of this; but he picked up seven sheep, stuffed them into his pocket, and ordered Karl to bring him seven more sheep in the morning, together with seven cheeses and a pailful of butter.

'And mind you come!' he roared.

'Oh, I shall come,' said Karl. 'I'm looking forward to it.'

'Ha! Ha! Ha! What? What? Are you indeed?' roared Jabor.

And he stamped away up the valley, which echoed to the tramp of his feet.

Next morning, there was young Karl going up to the castle with the seven sheep, and the seven cheeses, and the pailful of butter.

'Live together, or die together,' Karl was thinking. 'That's what I said, and that's what I mean. But I would to heaven we were all three well out of this!'

As yesterday, so today. Up at the castle the cauldron full of porridge was steaming over a fire in a corner of the courtyard, and Jabor was still in bed. Karl left the sheep in the courtyard, carried the butter and the cheeses up into the bedroom, and was told by Jabor to go and stir the porridge. Karl had a thought to let his brothers out of the stable – but then, what use in that? Jabor would only catch them again, and then he would surely kill them. 'I must kill *him*,' thought Karl. 'But how – how?'

And as he stood and stirred, and wondered desperately what he should do, there came a starling flying round over the porridge pot.

'Good morning, good morning!' said the starling. 'I could do with a beakful of that porridge, if it wasn't so hot!'

Then Karl tipped a ladleful of porridge on to the ground. 'It will soon cool, little bird,' he said. 'May you live happy!'

'May you live happy also,' said the starling.

'I think there is not much chance of that,' said Karl.

'Oh, never say die!' chirruped the starling, and he swallowed down the spoonful of porridge, and flew swiftly away. In less than no time he came flying back. He had a brown pebble in his beak. He laid the pebble at Karl's feet and said, 'Pick it up – put it in the cauldron.'

'Well, to please you,' said Karl. And he dropped the pebble into the cauldron. 'But what good will it do? You can't choke a monster with a pebble!'

'You'll see, you'll see!' chirruped the starling. And he flew up on to the courtyard wall.

By and by Jabor came stamping out. 'Is the porridge ready?' he roared.

'Yes,' said Karl.

'Not burned?' roared Jabor.

'No, not burned,' said Karl.

'We'll soon see about that!' roared Jabor. And he snatched the ladle out of Karl's hand, and crammed it dripping with porridge into his mouth. 'Good,' he said, 'good! We'll have another mouthful!'

But he was not to have another mouthful: for no sooner had he gulped once, than he gave a faint roar, and the ladle dropped from his hand. 'You – ' he stuttered. 'What – '

And that was the last word ever he spoke; for his eyes glazed and his limbs stiffened, and there he stood, no longer living, but turned to stone.

'Oh, my bird, my bird,' shouted Karl, 'you have saved our lives!'

And he ran to unbolt the stable door. 'Come out, my brothers, come out!' he shouted.

But even as Konrad and Fabian were stumbling out of the stable, the starling came flying.

'Not saved yet!' cried the starling. 'Don't you know that Jabor invited seven more monsters to feast with him today? Even now, even now, those seven monsters are tramping into the valley. Hurry! Hurry! Go into the castle kitchen, you will find seven iron pots there. Bring them here, fill them with porridge, carry them out of the courtyard, and put them in a row, one beyond the other, along the road outside the castle gates. If you are to save your lives, the monsters must all have a taste of that porridge!'

So Karl ran, and Konrad ran, and Fabian ran; they fetched the iron pots, they filled them with porridge, they carried them out of the courtyard and set them in a row, one beyond the other, along the road that led up to the castle gates. And all the time the starling flew round and round them, crying out, 'Hurry, lads, hurry!'

And scarcely had they set down the seven iron pots along the road, and gone back into the courtyard, when the earth shook and the hills echoed, and seven great monsters came stamping up out of the valley, one behind the other.

Stamp, stamp, stamp! Up came the seven monsters to where the seven pots of porridge stood by the roadside. And there they stopped and stared.

'Ha!' roared the leading monster. 'A pretty thought! Our friend Jabor welcomes us with a foretaste of the feast! Come, stand in line, my lads, and let us wish him good health in a gulp of porridge.'

So each monster took up a pot, and having roared out, 'Good health and good eating to our friend, Jabor!' they threw back their

83

heads, opened their great mouths, set the pots to their lips, and gulped down the porridge.

What happened? The pots dropped from their hands, their eyes glazed, their limbs stiffened: there they stood in line along the road, turned to stone.

'We are saved, we are saved, brothers!' cried Karl.

'We are saved, we are saved!' cried Konrad and Fabian.

'Yes, you are saved,' chirped the starling. 'Now the first thing to do is to make a bonfire and tip all the porridge into it, lest any of my friends should fancy a beakful. . . . And you'd better give the pebble back to me – it's a dangerous plaything to leave lying about.'

So Karl took the pebble out of the cauldron and gave it to the starling, who flew off with it. And then the three lads gathered a great pile of wood and set fire to it. And when the fire was burning merrily, they tipped all the porridge from the cauldron and from the iron pots into the flames. And after that, they let the sheep out of the stable and drove them down into the valley.

But they didn't stay long in their little cabin in the valley. Since there were now no monsters left in that part of the country, they took possession of Jabor's great castle, and there they lived ever after in great happiness – and proudly too. For there are not many castles in the world that can boast a stone monster in the courtyard; nor yet a procession of stone monsters on the road leading up to it.

And in the spring the starling came with his mate and built a nest on stone Jabor's head. There he brought up a brood of young ones, to whom he often told the story of the wonderful pebble. But in what secret place he kept the pebble – that he would never tell them. And to this day, no one but the starling knows where it is hidden.

9 · The Great Golloping Wolf

A young woodcutter, called Stepan, lived in a hut in the forest. And one wet and windy evening, when Stepan sat by the fire cooking broth for his supper, there came a timid knocking at the door.

Stepan took up a lantern and opened the door. Who stood outside? An old, old man dressed in rags, with the rain streaming over his bald head and running down his white beard.

'Shelter for the love of heaven!' gasped the old man, holding out a trembling hand.

Stepan took the old man's hand, led him in, sat him by the fire, took the dripping coat from off him, wrapped him in a blanket, dried his poor old head and his shaking hands with a towel, took off his leaky boots, and rubbed his cold feet with gentle hands. Then he emptied his supper broth into a basin, and said, 'Come, drink this up, and you will feel better!'

'No, no,' mumbled the old man. 'I cannot rob you of your supper.'

'Who talks of robbing?' laughed Stepan. 'I have had one good meal today, and I am not hungry. I can wait till morning. Then I will go out and shoot a rabbit for our breakfast.'

'*Our* breakfast?' faltered the old man.

'Yes, our breakfast,' said Stepan, 'for tonight you shall be my guest.'

So, when the old man had gobbled up the broth, Stepan put him to sleep in his own bed, and himself lay down by the hearth.

'Goodnight, my guest,' said he.

The old man didn't answer. He had fallen asleep.

Stepan fell asleep too. And when he woke in the morning – what did he see? No feeble old man, but a majestic wizard, wearing a robe that glowed with all the colours of the rainbow. The wizard clapped his hands, and, immediately, there on the table appeared a breakfast for two: such a delicious breakfast as Stepan had never tasted in all his life before.

'Oh!' laughed Stepan. 'I've heard of entertaining angels unawares!'

'No angel, Stepan,' said his guest. 'Just a grateful old wizard who

now offers you the choice between riches and a good wife. Which shall it be? Think carefully!'

'I don't need to think,' said Stepan. 'A good wife, if you please!'

The wizard went to the door and opened it. 'Come!' he said. 'Come, Stepan's wife!'

And in stepped a maiden lovely as a summer dawn.

Then the wizard, having blessed them both, went on his way And Stepan and the maiden, whose name was Melitsa, got married.

On the morning after their wedding, Melitsa said, 'My husband, are you content that I have brought you no marriage portion?'

'I am more than content, my wife,' said Stepan.

'But I am not content,' said Melitsa. And she went to stand outside the hut and clapped her hands.

What happened? The hut turned into a lovely little palace, with a golden roof and diamond doors and window frames. And all round the little palace, where the forest had been, lay beautiful flower gardens, and orchards where brightly coloured birds sang among the fruit-laden branches, and meadows where fallow deer wandered, and a little river flowed babbling among blossoming willows.

And in that palace, Stepan and Melitsa lived happily for a while.

But only for a while.

For of course the news of the wonderful little palace, that had appeared so suddenly, spread far and wide. And when the king, who was an old selfish widower, came to hear of it, he was angry. 'Who is this upstart lad, that he should own a palace finer than mine, and a wife more beautiful than any of my court ladies?' said the king to himself. 'Such a palace and such a wife should belong to *me*! I must get rid of that fellow!'

And he sent for Stepan and said, 'My lad, are you my faithful subject?'

'I hope I am, your majesty,' said Stepan.

'Then, my lad, I have an errand for you. I have heard that somewhere in the world is a flute that plays of itself the most marvellous music. Go, find me that self-playing flute, and I will greatly reward you. But if you refuse to go, or if you go and come back without finding the flute, then, Stepan, it grieves me to tell you that you must lose your head. Now be off with you! In the meantime I will take care of your palace for you – and of your lovely wife also.'

Well then – no good for Stepan to protest that he did not believe such a flute existed, and even if it did exist, how was it possible for him to find it without knowing which way to go seeking for it? All that happened was that the king flew into a most unkingly rage, shouted, stamped his foot, and swore that he would send for the executioner then and there if Stepan did not immediately set out.

So Stepan bowed low, and hurried off to tell Melitsa.

'It seems we have to part for a little while, my Stepan,' said

Melitsa. 'Go, cut me a switch from one of the willow trees that grow by the river.'

Stepan took a knife, went down to the river, cut a willow switch, and brought it to Melitsa. Then Melitsa gave him a little towel with her name embroidered on it, and said, 'When you wash, Stepan, use no other towel than this to dry your face. Come, keep up your spirits – the king shall not have our palace, nor shall he have me. And now goodbye, my Stepan.'

Then with the switch she struck the gate of the palace, and also struck herself. What happened? Where the castle had been, stood a stone mountain, and where Melitsa had been, stood a grey rock. And from the rock came a voice, 'When you return, my Stepan, lay your hand upon me and call me forth. And if you do not return. . . .'

But Stepan heard no more. He turned and fled away. And the tears ran down his face.

He went, went, went, asking everyone he met where he could find the self-playing flute. But no one could tell him. He went for days, he went for weeks, he went for months, he went till his shoes were in holes and his clothes in rags. And he came one evening to a great house, standing on pillars shaped like hen's legs.

At the door of the house stood an old woman, who hailed him and said, 'Whither away, my handsome youth? Whither away so fast, and all in rags?'

'I go to seek the self-playing flute, little mother,' said Stepan. 'If you can give me news of it?'

'I cannot give you news of it,' said the old woman. 'But my master, the Great Golloping Wolf – ah, he's a wise one who knows many strange things! He may be able to tell us. Come in and wait – he'll be home directly, and I will ask him. But I must hide you; yes, I must hide you, for if he comes home hungry, I can't say but what he will swallow you down at one gulp. Hark, here he comes! Get behind the stove, and hold yourself still and silent.'

Well, Stepan had hardly crouched down behind the stove, when – *whizz! bang!* – in whirled the Great Golloping Wolf. My word, but he was a monster! He had a wolf's head, with the brightest and fiercest eyes that ever rolled in any creature's head. His body was

88

that of a giant, with long hairy arms and clawed hands and feet. And when he stood erect, his head banged against the ceiling and made holes in it.

Sniff, sniff, sniff went the hairy nose of the Great Golloping Wolf. And he roared out:

> *'Well, well,*
> *I smell, I smell,*
> *What do I smell?*
> *The blood of a human mannikin!'*

'At it again!' said the old woman. 'You and your nose! Always smelling out something that isn't there. Come, you stupid old golloper, take your supper – it's in the cauldron.'

The Great Golloping Wolf made a snatch at the cauldron that was bubbling on the fire, raised it high above his head, and swallowed all that was in it at one gulp. Then he set down the cauldron, sniffed again, looked behind the stove, grabbed up Stepan, whirled him over his head, and roared out:

> *'Ho! Ho!*
> *Told you so!*
> *And here's the human mannikin!'*

'Oh, what a pretty little pickaninny! Well for you, my pretty, that I'm full. But I shall be empty tomorrow.'

Then he set Stepan down on the floor, peered at him closely, and said, 'What's the use of you? Can you play cards? Afraid of me, are you?'

'Yes, I can play cards,' answered Stepan boldly. 'And I am *not* afraid of you.'

'Well, never mind,' laughed the Great Golloping Wolf. 'Tonight you shall play with me; tomorrow you shall feed me. Old woman, bring out the cards. I like a game of cards,' he explained. 'But I can't play with the old woman, she doesn't know one card from another, and she cheats – oh oh, how she cheats! Do you cheat, my pickaninny?'

'No, I do not,' said Stepan. 'But I've come a long way. I'm very tired, and very hungry.'

'Old woman,' roared the Great Golloping Wolf, 'is there aught in the pantry?'

'There's some apple pie,' said the old woman.

'Then bring it out, old woman, bring it out, and let the pickaninny eat. We won't starve him, no, no, we won't starve him! We've got a very tender heart! Haven't we, old woman, haven't we, eh?'

'Oh, stop your nonsense!' said the old woman. 'I've known softer hearts than yours!'

She fetched the apple tart and Stepan ate it, and the Great Golloping Wolf watched him and laughed. Then he sat down at the table, and Stepan sat opposite him, and the Great Golloping Wolf dealt out the cards. But when he caught Stepan yawning (for indeed Stepan was so tired he could scarcely keep his eyes open) the Great Golloper roared out, 'You mustn't fall asleep! I can't have you falling asleep! If you do fall asleep I shall swallow you!'

'I shouldn't think of falling asleep,' said Stepan.

And they began to play.

It should have been a simple enough game, being none other than Snap. The cards were big and brightly coloured, and very curious – pictures of queer faces, and writhing serpents and all manner of strange beasts. But what was queerer than queer was that the pictures on the cards kept moving and changing: first the faces were grinning, then they were scowling; the serpents hissed and wriggled and turned into bats, and back again into serpents; and as to the rest of the pictured beasts, they never kept still for a moment – they were elephants, they were lions, they were crocodiles, they were tigers. And each card, as Stepan set it down, growled, or roared, or trumpeted, or squealed. And every time Stepan said 'Snap!' it wasn't snap at all, because the picture on the card he put down had turned into something else.

But the strange behaviour of the cards didn't seem to trouble the Great Golloping Wolf. It was 'Snap, snap, snap!' with him, and shovelling up the cards, and beating Stepan hollow. That didn't matter. In fact it was good in a way, because it kept the monster in a good temper. But what did matter, was that Stepan felt so very, very sleepy. His eyes kept closing, and his head kept nodding; and then the old woman, who stood behind the chair watching the game, would give him a pinch, and he would blink and cough and sit up straight again. But by and by – oh dear me! – even the old woman's pinches failed to rouse him, and he had actually begun to dream that he was back in his palace with Melitsa, when he was jerked wide awake by the monster's angry roar. 'You sleep! You sleep! And now I *shall* gulp you down!'

'I do *not* sleep,' said Stepan. 'I just closed my eyes in order to think more clearly.'

'Well then, what were you thinking?'

'I was thinking,' said Stepan, 'that I have walked through many dense forests in my journeying, and everywhere I saw more crooked trees than straight ones.'

'I don't believe it!' said the Great Golloping Wolf.

'But I assure you it is so,' said Stepan.

'Wait! Wait! I must see into this!' shouted the Great Golloping Wolf. And he sprang up and ran out of the house. 'If you've lied to me, I'll gulp you down the moment I come back!' he roared, as he hurried away.

The old woman chuckled. 'Take a bit of a doze now, clever lad,' said she. 'Trust me to give you a nudge, soon as I hear my Great Golloper coming back.'

So, whilst the Great Golloping Wolf was rushing through all the forests of the world, faster than any whirlwind, with trees, both straight and crooked, crashing round him, Stepan sat sprawled among the curious cards, and slept.

But he sat up straight and very wide awake when by and by the old woman pinched the back of his neck, just as the Great Golloping Wolf came stamping into the house, shouting, 'You're right, my pickaninny, you're right, I've counted all the trees in the world, and there *are* more crooked ones. Now I shan't have to swallow you, and we can get on with the game!'

So they took up the cards again; and it was 'Snap, snap, snap!' on the monster's part, and yawn, yawn, yawn on Stepan's, and his head nodding, and his eyes closing, and jerking himself awake when the old woman gave him a pinch . . . and his eyes closing again, until – oh dear – there he was asleep again, and starting awake again at the angry roar of the Great Golloping Wolf, 'You sleep! You sleep!'

'I do *not* sleep!' said Stepan. 'I am wide awake! I was thinking a thought.'

'What thought were you thinking this time?' shouted the Great Golloper.

'I was thinking,' said Stepan, 'that in my travels I have crossed many rivers and I have sailed over many seas, and everywhere I saw more small fish than big ones.'

'That may be true, and it may not be true,' said the monster. 'I shall go and see for myself. If it is *not* true, I'll gollop you down! Yes, I'll gollop you down!'

And he rushed out of the house.

Again Stepan slept with his head on the table, and again he was wakened by the old woman's pinches just as the Great Golloper came back, with his hairy body adrip from the seas and rivers he had waded through.

'You're right again!' shouted the monster. 'There *are* more small fish. You're wise, my little pickaninny, you're wise!' And they went on playing cards.

But it wasn't long before Stepan was yawning and blinking again. And though he struggled hard to keep awake, it was no good: his head nodded, his eyes closed, and this time he fell so fast asleep that the old woman's sly pinches failed to wake him. What did wake him was the monster's grabbing the back of his coat in his long teeth, swinging him into the air, shaking him like a terrier shaking a rat, and then dropping him with a bump on to the floor.

'Now I *shall* eat you,' roared the monster. 'I shall crunch you up with all your little bones!'

Oh me! What was Stepan to do now? If only he could gain a little time, he might think of some way out! So he said, 'Ah my lord, Great Golloper, you see how very dirty and dusty and travel-stained I am. If you would allow me to wash before you swallowed me, I think I should taste the sweeter.'

'So you would!' said the monster. 'Old woman, take the little rascal into the scullery, fill the wash tub, give him some soap. But mind you, pickaninny, you must be quick with your washing. No dawdling! I feel my mouth beginning to water for pickaninny flesh!'

So the old woman took Stepan into the scullery, filled the wash tub with warm water, gave him a cake of soap. 'Oh, my handsome!' she said. 'Oh, my handsome, that it should come to this!'

And she burst out crying, and left him.

You may be sure Stepan didn't hurry over his bath. He took as long as ever he could, and all the time he was racking his brains to think of some way of escape. But there was no window in the scullery, and no way out except back through the kitchen, where the monster was prowling up and down. And the monster was getting impatient! Every now and then he would shout, 'Haven't you finished washing? Haven't you finished washing?'

'Very nearly,' answered Stepan. 'Just another minute or two!'

And at last the monster flung open the scullery door and shouted, 'I'm not going to wait any longer!'

So Stepan got out of the bath, and the monster flung a towel at him.

'Here, take this, dry yourself, and be quick about it!' growled the monster.

Stepan took up the towel. Then he laid it down again. He remembered Melitsa putting the little embroidered towel into his hands and saying, 'When you wash, my Stepan, use no other towel than this to dry your face.'

'Thank you, but I have my own towel,' he said. And he took Melitsa's towel out of his coat pocket.

The Great Golloping Wolf stared. He snatched the towel out of Stepan's hand, he held it close to his fiery eyes, turned it this way and that way. 'Where did you get this towel?' he roared.

'My wife gave it to me,' said Stepan.

'What! Your *wife!* Why didn't you say so before?' shouted the monster. 'That's Melitsa's towel! My dear little sister Melitsa's towel! Think of it, you stupid pickaninny – I was just about to eat you! Yes, just about to gollop down my own brother-in-law! And where is my little sister Melitsa, and how is my little sister Melitsa? Come, dry yourself quickly, put on your rags; we'll sit by the fire, and you shall tell me all about it.'

So Stepan hurried to dry and dress; and very soon he and the monster were sitting in friendly fashion by the kitchen fire, and Stepan was telling the monster all about everything, from the night when the old magician came into his hut, to this night. And when the tale was told the monster said, 'Wait a minute! Wait a minute! *I* know where the self-playing flute is. I'll get it for you in a jiffy!'

And he rushed out of the house again.

See now, the monster's off across the world. Sometimes he's leaping over the earth, sometimes he's bounding through the air. He's speeding over the mountains, he's racing through the valleys, he's crashing through forests, he's wading through rivers, he's plunging through seas; and beyond the thrice-nine-land in the thirtieth kingdom he gives a jump over a high stone wall, and comes down in an orchard full of apple trees. And on one of those trees, among the ripe rosy apples, the self-playing flute hangs swinging from fifty golden chains.

The Great Golloper Wolf reaches up a hairy hand, he snaps the gold chains one after the other, he snatches the self-playing flute: one leap and he's back over the high stone wall, with the self-playing flute held in his long teeth.

But now the lord of the thirtieth kingdom, the owner of the flute, a ghost in a cloudy shirt, is after him, screaming out threats and curses, spitting out trails of mist that coil themselves about the feet of the Great Golloping Wolf, and seek to trip him up.

The Great Golloping Wolf kicks away the mists and races on. He comes to the ocean, he plunges in, he holds his head high above the breakers, and the self-playing flute is safe between his teeth.

The lord of the thirtieth kingdom, the misty ghost, the owner of the self-playing flute, plunges into the ocean also. But the billows rise up over him, he sinks down, down among the billows; mists cover the face of the ocean, the lord of the thirtieth kingdom is sucked down to the ocean floor. And the monster, the Great Golloping Wolf, holding the self-playing flute between his long teeth, wades safely ashore, speeds back over the mountains, and along the valleys, and through the forests. Puffing and panting he reaches his great house, and with a roar of triumph flings down the self-playing flute at Stepan's feet.

'There, brother-in-law!' he shouts. 'Now you shall go to bed and sleep. Tomorrow you shall go home, and I will go behind you!'

Who but Stepan was happy now? The old woman made up a bed for him, and he slept that night without a care; and early next morning set off on his journey home, with the self-playing flute tucked in his coat pocket, and the Great Golloping Wolf following after him like any friendly dog.

It was a happy journey. When Stepan wearied the Great Golloping Wolf took him up on his back; and when Stepan hungered and thirsted, the Great Golloping Wolf snapped his clawed fingers, and meat and drink appeared. And every now and then the Great Golloper would be chuckling to himself and saying, 'Soon now I shall see my little sister Melitsa, my little fairy sister Melitsa! I shall take her in my arms, and she will kiss my hairy snout. My little sister Melitsa is not afraid of her ugly brother! She loves him, and he loves her!'

But when they came to the stone mountain that had once been Stepan's palace, and to the grey rock that had once been Melitsa, the Great Golloping Wolf lay down on the bare ground and howled.

'My little sister Melitsa,' he howled, 'my little sister Melitsa! Is it to greet a grey rock that I have travelled all this weary way?'

Then Stepan remembered Melitsa's words, 'When you return, my Stepan, lay your hand upon me and call me forth. And if you do not return. . . .'

'But I *have* returned, Melitsa, my darling!' cried Stepan, 'I have returned, and the self-playing flute is in my pocket! So now I call you! Come forth, Melitsa, my darling! Come forth!'

And no sooner had Stepan spoken those words than the grey rock vanished: and there stood Melitsa, lovely as a summer dawn, and laughing.

'Stepan, my dear, dear husband!'

'Melitsa, my darling wife!'

There they were in each others arms.

'Oh ho! Oh ho!' The Great Golloping Wolf went wild with joy. He caught up Melitsa, he caught up Stepan, he hugged them both, trying to be gentle, but not succeeding very well. And when he set them down, Melitsa stepped to the great stone mountain and touched the base of it with her white hand. And the mountain sank, sank, down into the earth, and up from the earth rose the beautiful little palace with the golden roof and the diamond window panes. And all round the palace the bare earth blossomed: there once more were the beautiful flower gardens, and the orchards where brightly coloured birds sang on the fruit-laden branches; there were the meadows where fallow deer roamed, and there was the little river that flowed babbling among blossoming willows.

Hand in hand Stepan and Melitsa went into the palace. And the Great Golloping Wolf went down on all fours, and followed them in like a dog.

So that day they rejoiced together, and next morning the Great Golloping Wolf bade them goodbye and went back to his own home. And Stepan and Melitsa, dressed in their best, set out for the city, to carry the self-playing flute to the king.

The king wasn't at all pleased to see them. He scowled at the flute and said, 'Bah! Would you palm me off with this common instrument? *This* is no self-playing flute!' And he flung the flute on the floor, shouting, 'Now play if you can! Play if you can!'

And the flute began to play. It played such a merry, merry tune that the king laughed, jumped down from the throne, took the leading court lady by the hand, and began to dance. The court gentlemen laughed, the court ladies laughed, they joined hands and danced round the king. They laughed and danced, laughed and danced. And Stepan and Melitsa laughed also, and danced with the rest. Never was seen a gayer, happier throng: they danced till they were weary with dancing, they laughed till they had no breath left; the king fell back exhausted on to his throne, and, still laughing, panted out, 'Enough! Enough!'

Then the flute ceased playing. And the king, being now in a

thoroughly good temper, forgot that he had ever envied Stepan his golden palace and his lovely wife. In fact, he then and there made Stepan a duke.

All the court ladies clapped their hands; all the court gentlemen shouted 'Hurrah!' Duke Stepan bowed, Duchess Melitsa curtseyed. Hand in hand they went back to their golden palace. And in that golden palace they lived happily ever after.

10 · The Seven Monsters

Well, there were seven monsters, and there was the king's daughter.

The king's daughter was out walking with her six friends. The monsters were hiding in a cave. The girls passed by the cave, and the monsters saw them.

'Ah ha! Here comes our dinner! A tender little maiden for each one of us!'

But which monster is to eat the king's daughter? 'Me! me! me! me! me! me! me!' The monsters began quarrelling. The girls heard them; they ran, ran.

'Catch them, boys! After them, boys!' The monsters came out of the cave. They ran, ran, after the girls.

The girls were running, the monsters were running; the monsters ran faster than the girls. Oh me, what can the girls do? They see a tall tree, they scramble up among the branches, up and up.

The monsters tried to climb up after them, but they were too heavy, they broke the tree branches, they fell to the ground. They stood under the tree and howled.

Said Monster Slobber, 'We must cut down the tree!'

Said Monster Yellow Belly to Monster Snaggle Tooth, 'You go home and fetch an axe.'

Said Monster Snaggle Tooth, 'No, I won't go. The girls may tumble out of the tree before I get back, and then *you* will eat the king's daughter.'

'Short Shanks, *you* go!'

'No, I won't – go yourself!'

'Goggle Eyes, you go!'

'No!'

'Dish Face, you go!'

'No!'

'Blue Nose, you go!'

'No, no, *no!*'

'Well then, we must all go.'

And they hurried off, all seven of them, to fetch the axe.

Then the girls took off their dresses and hung them among the tree branches. They came down from the tree in their shifts and ran on. The monsters came back with the axe. They looked up into the tree and saw the dresses. 'Ah, the girls are still up there!' They began to cut down the tree.

The girls were running, running. They came to a great rock.

'Oh Rock, thou art our father and our mother, shelter us!'

The Rock opened itself. The girls crept inside. The Rock closed itself behind them.

Chop, chop, chop! The monsters were hacking at the tree. The tree creaked, the tree groaned, the tree fell. What's this? Only a scatter of clothes among the branches! 'Ah, ha, the girls have deceived us! Which way have they gone? See – their footprints in the soft ground! This way! This way!'

The monsters run in the track of the footprints. They come to the Rock. No more footprints! Then the girls are inside the Rock.

'Rock! Rock! Open yourself!'

'No, not I!'

Said Monster Slobber, 'We must split Rock open! You, Yellow Belly, go home and fetch the stone hammer.'

'No!'

'You go, Snaggle Tooth.'

'No!'

'You go, Goggle Eyes.'

'No!'

'You go, Dish Face.'

'No!'

'You go, Blue Nose!'

'No!'

'You go, Short Shanks.'

99

'No! No! *No!* The girls may come out before I get back, and then *you* will eat the king's daughter!'

'Well then,' says Monster Slobber, 'seems we must all go.'

So the seven monsters run home to fetch the stone hammer.

And the Rock said to the girls, 'You had better come out now.'

Then the Rock opened itself. The girls came out. They ran on.

The monsters came back with the stone hammer. The Rock said, 'It's no good hammering at me. The girls have gone this long while.'

The monsters flung the stone hammer at the Rock. They howled and ran on after the girls. The girls were running now across an open plain. They looked back. Oh me, there come the monsters! No shelter on this plain! Where to hide? But see, there are some reeds, and in the reeds sits Toad.

'Oh Toad, thou art our father and our mother – hide us!'

Toad says, 'You are a big mouthful, but I will do my best.'

Toad swells himself, and swells himself. He opens his mouth. He swallows all the girls. There they are now, safe inside his stomach.

Then Toad fills his cheeks with leaden bullets. Where did he get those bullets from? From his store house under the reeds. Toad has been collecting leaden bullets out of the marsh for a long time.

Now come the monsters, yelling and threatening. 'Toad, give us the girls you have swallowed! Spit them out, or it will be the worse for you!'

Toad says, 'All right. Don't make a fuss. But stand in line.'

The monsters stand in line. Monster Slobber is leading.

Toad opens his mouth. He spits bullets out of his cheek.

De-de! Monster Slobber and Monster Yellow Belly fall dead.

The other monsters cry, 'No, no, no! Spit out the king's daughter!'

Toad says, 'Very well. But keep quiet. Stand in line.'

The five other monsters stand in line. Toad opens his mouth. He spits some more bullets out of his cheek. *De-de-de-de-de!* All the other monsters fall dead.

Toad comes out of the reeds. He goes to the king's village; he sits by the king's well.

The women come to fetch water for the king.

Toad says, 'Take a message to the king. Tell him to spread a blue carpet from this well to his house.'

The women take the message. The king's men come with the blue carpet, they spread it out. Toad sits on the edge of the carpet. He opens his mouth, he spits out the king's daughter, he spits out all the girls. The girls run merrily along the blue carpet to the king's house. The king gives a feast. Now the girls are eating sweet cakes. The king's men carry some sweet cakes to Toad.

And the king has a golden crown made for Toad to wear when he sits among the reeds.

11 · The Singing Leaves

A merchant had three pretty daughters; and one day, as he was setting out on business to a distant city, he called his daughters to him and said, 'My dears, if my affairs prosper I will bring home a present for each of you. Choose now what those presents shall be.'

The eldest girl said, 'Dear Father, I should like a diamond necklace.'

The second girl said, 'I should like a pearl-studded waistband.'

But the youngest, whose name was Zelinda, said nothing.

'Well, my little one?' said the merchant.

'Dear Father,' said Zelinda then, 'you have given me so many pretty things that I seem to have nothing left to wish for.'

'But you must choose *something*,' said the merchant. 'I cannot bring presents to your sisters and leave you out.'

Then Zelinda laughed and said, 'I have heard that somewhere in the world there is a tree whose leaves sing and dance. If in your travels you should come across that tree, bring me a leaf.'

'So I will,' said the merchant; and he also laughed, kissed the three girls goodbye, got on his horse, and rode off.

Well, the merchant prospered in his business; and before he left the city to return home, he bought the diamond necklace for his eldest girl, and the pearl-studded waistband for the second girl. But when he inquired of his fellow merchants if they could tell him where he could find the tree with the singing leaves, they said, 'That's nothing but an old fairy tale. Such a tree doesn't exist.'

'I was afraid it didn't,' said the merchant. And he bought a pretty brooch for his youngest daughter, and set out on his ride home.

Now the weather had turned stormy and cold. And he hadn't ridden far before it began to snow. And as the snow fell thicker and thicker, covering the roads and blotting out the familiar landmarks, the merchant lost his way. To make matters worse, it was already evening, he was still far from home, and nowhere could he see an inn or any house where he might seek shelter for the night. So he let the reins go slack, trusting to his good horse to find a way where he couldn't.

And his good horse did find a way. All at once, through a belt of trees on his right hand, the merchant saw a brilliant light shining; and making towards the light, it wasn't long before he came to the wide open gates of a castle. And from every window of that castle light was streaming out into the snowy darkness.

'Ah, my good horse, I did well to trust you!' said the merchant. And he rode up to the great door of the castle, dismounted and knocked.

Knock, knock, knock.

No answer.

Knock, knock, knock again.

No answer.

'But surely *someone* must be here!' thought the merchant. And finding the door was not locked, he pushed it open, and stepped inside.

'Anyone at home?'

No answer.

But see – in a little room that opened out of the great hall, a bright fire burning, and a table laid with meat and bread and fruit and wine.

The merchant was very hungry, and very cold. He longed to sit down and warm himself, and eat and drink. But first he must see to his horse. So he went back into the courtyard. No horse! Oh dear me, what could have happened? He stood for a moment dazzled by the falling snow, which sparkled in the lights that streamed from the castle windows. Then he heard a gentle whinnying, and crossing the court, came to the half-open door of a stable.

Into the stable he went, and there in a loose box, with a rackful

of hay and a manger full of oats, he found his horse, unharnessed
and rubbed down, standing on a thick bed of straw and contentedly
munching.

'Am I awake, or can this all be a dream?' thought the merchant.

But if it was a dream, it was a very pleasant one. So he said
goodnight to his horse, and went back into the castle, to the little
room where the fire blazed and the food waited. And there he sat
before the fire and warmed himself, and ate and drank.

And after that, he fell asleep.

When he woke in the morning – where did he find himself?
In bed in a charming room, wearing a sleeping robe of soft warm
velvet. His clothes, dried and brushed, were neatly folded on a
chair, and a bath of warm water stood at the end of the bed. So
he got up, washed and dressed himself, and went back to the
little room off the great hall, where he found breakfast waiting
for him. But still, in all that great castle, there seemed to be no
living soul except himself.

So, having breakfasted, he tore a leaf from his pocket book,
and wrote a note: *To my unseen host, a thousand grateful thanks from
a weary traveller*. He laid the note on the table, and went out into
the courtyard. The sun was shining brilliantly in a clear sky; the
snow had been swept from the court, and lay in glistening heaps
under the walls. In the stable his horse stood ready saddled and
bridled, and whinnying with pleasure at the sight of him.

'What a tale I shall have to tell to my three girls when I get
home!' thought the merchant. And he mounted his horse and rode
off through the open courtyard gates, and down through an avenue
of tall leafless trees.

Clipperty-clop! Clipperty-clop! The trotting hoofs sounding
merrily in the morning stillness. But what was that other sound?
A strain of sweetest music that seemed to come from beyond a
wooded grove on the merchant's right hand. Curious as the merchant
felt, he would have ridden past that grove, so eager was he to get
home; but the horse thought differently, and willy-nilly turned
into the grove and cantered down it. Now, high over the merchant's
head, graceful trees arched their bare and frost-sparkling branches,

silent, motionless; but still from somewhere beyond them came that sweet music, and a sound of singing too, as if a choir of fairy voices sang in an unknown tongue to the accompaniment of fairy instruments.

And then – there at the end of the grove, in a little garden bright with flowers, the merchant saw it: the singing tree, whose every leaf, green and fresh as in high summer, danced in the still air – and dancing, sang.

'So you are not a fairy tale after all,' said the merchant, 'and my little Zelinda shall have her singing leaf!'

And he stood in the stirrups, reached up, and picked a leaf.

For a moment he heard the leaf singing in his hand, but the next moment the leaf's music was drowned in a roar of rage, and a monster – so hideous that nothing more hideous has ever been seen on earth – came striding into the garden.

'Thief!' roared the monster. 'Is this the way you repay my hospitality? Have I not fed you, bedded you, warmed you, welcomed you, and do you now think to rob me?' And he seized the merchant in his great fist, dragged him from his horse, and shook him till his teeth rattled.

Then he opened his hand, and the merchant fell on his knees.

'Oh, my gracious lord,' stammered the merchant, 'I meant no harm. I only picked one leaf – just one – for my little daughter. She – she asked me, gracious lord, before I left home to – to bring her. . . .'

And stuttering with fright, the merchant told the monster about his three daughters, and about the presents he had promised to bring them, and how Zelinda had said she wanted nothing; and then had laughed and asked for a singing leaf, if by chance he should find one. 'And oh, my gracious lord,' he stammered, 'she is such a darling little modest maiden, so good, so kind, so beautiful, that if you were to see her you could deny her nothing!'

'Get up, you fool,' said the monster, but less roughly. 'Don't kneel to me! Standing or kneeling I can squeeze the life out of you if I so please. But I will spare you, on one condition – that you bring me this treasure of a daughter.'

The merchant sprang to his feet. Now he felt afraid no longer, he blazed with indignation. 'Am I so poor a thing,' he cried, 'that I would save my own life at the expense of my daughter's? No, I will *not* bring you my Zelinda! Now, kill me if you will!'

'Yet you will bring her,' said the monster. 'Because you must. Otherwise I shall come and fetch her; and *if* I come, I will drag your house about your ears, and bury the lot of you in the ruins. Now, up on your horse and go, before I change my mind and throttle you!'

Then the monster stepped over the garden wall and strode off. And the merchant, scarcely conscious of what he was doing, got on his horse and rode home. As to the singing leaf, he thought to throw it away, but it stayed clinging to his hand, and all the way home it sang, sometimes sadly, sometimes happily. And when it sang sadly, the merchant thought his heart would break; but when it sang happily, it seemed to him that perhaps all might yet be well.

But when he got home the leaf was silent; and for a little while the merchant was silent also, for he did not know how to tell his daughters what had befallen him. He gave the eldest girl her diamond necklace, he gave the middle daughter her pearl-studded waist-band, he gave Zelinda the pretty brooch he had bought for her. 'But I have something else for you, my little one,' he said. And he put the singing leaf in her hand, burst into tears, and told all that had happened.

Well there, what a scene! Zelinda's two sisters began to weep also, flinging their arms first round their father and then round Zelinda, crying out that it mustn't be, and it couldn't be, but oh, oh, oh, what if the monster should come as he had threatened, and kill them all? And oh, oh, oh, couldn't they all run away – far away into another country? They were quite wild with fear and grief.

But Zelinda stood quietly, holding the leaf in her hand. And when the hubbub had died down somewhat, she gave a sad little smile and said, 'It seems we have no choice left to us. Either I go to the monster, or the monster comes here and destroys us all. Of course I must go. I will pack up a few things now, so that I shall be ready to start first thing in the morning.' Then she kissed her father and went up to her room.

There she stood now, looking down at the leaf in her hand, that sparkled green and glittering in the candlelight.

'You have cost us very dear, my leaf,' she said.

And what did the leaf do? It gave a little tinkling laugh, and fluttered up and away through the open window, singing as it went.

'I shall never sleep tonight,' thought Zelinda.

But sleep she did, and soundly; and dreamed she was standing in a beautiful little garden, hand in hand with a handsome prince.

'Oh me,' thought Zelinda when she woke in the morning, 'they say dreams go by contraries. And where shall I be tonight – if I am still alive? But I must be brave, for all our sakes!'

Breakfast was a sad meal: nobody felt like eating anything. Zelinda's sisters were sobbing, her father sat pale and rigid; he seemed suddenly to have become an aged man. Zelinda tried to cheer him, but soon she was weeping herself; and when a man-servant came in to say that the horse was saddled and bridled and waiting at the door, the sisters clung to Zelinda crying, 'Don't go! Don't go!'

'You know I must go,' said Zelinda sadly. 'Goodbye, my darlings.' And she kissed them and went out with her father, who, saying no word, lifted her on to the horse, got up behind her, and rode away.

It was evening before they came to the end of their journey. The monster's castle was all brilliantly lighted up, as it had been when the merchant first saw it. And again, as soon as they alighted, the horse trotted off to the stable, to find his loose box prepared for him with food and drink and a bed of straw, and invisible hands to unharness him and rub him down. 'This is a very good place to come to,' said the horse to himself, as he munched contentedly.

Meanwhile Zelinda and her father had gone into the castle, where, in the little room that opened out of the great hall, a fire blazed on the hearth and the table was laid for two, with meat and bread and fruit and wine. Having eaten nothing all day, they were both very hungry. 'And even if it is to be our last meal together, dear Father, we may as well enjoy it,' said Zelinda. 'You shall eat for my sake, and I will eat for yours.'

So they ate and drank, and felt all the better for it. But they had scarcely finished their meal when the walls shook and the dishes rattled, the door flew open, and in tramped the monster.

'Good evening, merchant,' bellowed the monster. 'Well for you that you have kept your promise! Good evening, Zelinda. Have you come willingly, and are you prepared to stay?'

'Yes, I have come willingly, and I am prepared to stay,' answered Zelinda.

'Then you will find your beds prepared for you,' roared the monster. 'A bell will wake you in the morning. You, merchant, will leave first thing after your breakfast. I shall not be seeing you again. You shall not go home empty handed. You will find a pack horse carrying a chest full of gold in the courtyard, waiting to accompany you. But if you are not gone by ten o'clock, you will not be alive by eleven. Goodnight to you both.'

Then the monster stamped out again, slamming the door behind him.

'It seems I am not to be eaten tonight,' said Zelinda, trying to laugh. 'But you are very tired, dear Father. Come, let us go and look for our bedrooms.'

So they went, hand in hand, to open one door after another in that great castle, where they saw no one, and where they heard no sound but the muffled tread of their own footsteps on the richly carpeted floors. And by and by they came to two bedrooms, opening one out of the other, and elegantly furnished.

So they kissed each other goodnight and went to bed. What the merchant dreamed I can't tell you; but Zelinda again dreamed of the beautiful little garden and of the handsome prince, with whom she was walking hand in hand; and so she was happy in her sleep, even if she must wake unhappy at the clanging of a loud bell that seemed to bring all her fears crowding back upon her.

When she was dressed and had gone into the little room where breakfast was laid, she found her father in a sorry state, unable to eat, one moment saying he must be off, and the next moment declaring that he could not and would not leave her. And when at last Zelinda had persuaded him out into the courtyard, where beside his own horse, saddled and bridled, there stood a pack horse laden with a chest full of gold, he declared that the gold was the price of Zelinda's life, and that he would have none of it.

'But, dear Father,' said Zelinda, 'we must not offend the monster.'

So then her father leaped on to his horse, snatched up the pack horse's rein, gave a great cry, and rode off at a gallop.

'Now I am alone, quite quite alone,' thought Zelinda. 'But I must try to be brave and not cry.' Nevertheless she did shed a few tears as she went back into the castle, where everything was so silent and empty that the world seemed to be holding its breath. Where was she to go, what was she to do?

She wandered through the great hall and along a thickly carpeted corridor. There were many doors on each side of the corridor, but they were all shut and she did not dare to open them. But then at the end of the corridor she came to a door that was slightly ajar; and over the door in gold letters she read the words *Zelinda the Empress*, so she pushed the door open, and went in. Now she was in a beautiful little drawing-room, with flowers on the table, pictures on the walls, and shelves full of books. She took down a book, opened it, and saw on the title page the same words: *Zelinda the Empress*. What could it mean? She opened another book, and yet another, and in every one the same words: *Zelinda the Empress*. She felt frightened, ran out of the room, and came into the bedroom where she had slept last night. On the dressing table lay a ring, set with a sparkling diamond. She picked it up and looked at it. There in tiny letters, engraved on the golden circle – the same words: *Zelinda the Empress*. She glanced at the wardrobe: the same words carved along the beading: *Zelinda the Empress*. She opened the wardrobe which was full of the most beautiful dresses, and inside the neckband of each dress – those words again: *Zelinda the Empress*.

Oh, what *could* it mean? Was it kindness on the monster's part – or was it mockery? 'At any rate if I am Zelinda, I am certainly *not* an empress,' she thought, quickly shutting the wardrobe door, lest she be tempted to try on one of the beautiful dresses. And glancing up, she saw, hanging on the wall, a picture, where assuredly no picture had been a moment ago. And what was the picture but a portrait of the handsome prince she had dreamed of last night! The prince was standing under a tree in the little garden she had seen in her dream; and surely, surely he smiled and nodded to her. But next moment the picture faded and the room faded, and Zelinda was in the garden herself, standing under a tree whose leaves, stirred by a gentle breeze, danced and sang. 'Zelinda the Empress,' they sang, and, singing, laughed.

So all day she roamed about both outside and inside the castle, and saw more wonderful things than you can imagine, or I can tell of: an aviary full of brilliantly coloured birds who talked to her and told her to be happy; and then a room full of musical instruments that made music of themselves for her delight; and then a mirror hung against a wall in which she saw her home, and her father riding up to the front door, and her sisters coming out to greet him, and the pack horse being unloaded, and her sisters opening the chest that was full of gold coins. 'Oh if you would but smile, if you would but smile, dear Father,' said Zelinda to the image in the mirror, 'I could be quite, quite happy!'

But the father that she saw in the mirror did not smile. He went into the house, sat down with his elbows on the table, and his hands before his face, and wept.

Then Zelinda wept a little also. But at any rate all her fears had left her, for she felt sure now that the monster could not mean to kill her. So she dried her eyes and went into the room opening off the hall, where she found a tempting meal awaiting her. Now the sun had set, and the castle was lighting itself up: from every window lights streamed out into the dusky courtyard, and in the room where Zelinda sat, wax candles in diamond candlesticks were lighted by invisible hands, and burned with steady flames.

'If it is a dream,' thought Zelinda, 'it is all so wonderful that I could scarcely wish to wake.'

And then, just as she had finished her meal – oh dear – *stamp,*

stamp, stamp outside the room, the door burst open, and there stood the monster.

'Good evening, Zelinda,' roared the monster, in a voice which he seemed to be trying to make gentle, and which yet set the dishes on the table clattering, and made Zelinda tremble.

'Good evening, my lord.'

'Have you everything you want, Zelinda?'

'Yes, I have everything I want, my lord.'

'And are you happy, Zelinda?'

'No, I do not think I am very happy, my lord. But I am grateful.'

'Grateful, Zelinda – to me?'

'Yes, my lord.'

'Then Zelinda, will you marry me?'

'Oh, my lord, what can I say?'

'Say yes or no!' roared the monster.

'No, my lord.'

'Bah!' shouted the monster, and stamped out of the room, leaving Zelinda in tears.

That night Zelinda again dreamed of her handsome prince, but it was a sad dream. For the handsome prince spoke to her in the very words of the monster, 'Zelinda, will you marry me?' And when she answered 'How can I marry a dream?' he gave her an unhappy look and vanished.

Then it seemed to Zelinda that she ran seeking him, both inside and outside the castle, through room after room, and through garden after garden; but nowhere could she find him. And she awoke in tears.

Well, day after day went by in the same manner. Through the hours of daylight Zelinda saw no one, and amused herself as best she could, finding many strange and beautiful things inside the castle, and wandering out to sit under the singing tree and listen to its music. Every evening the monster came to visit her; and because she had no other company she came to look forward to his visits, even though sometimes he roared at her and frightened her. But most often now he was gentle and kind. Only every evening, before he left her, he asked her the same question, 'Zelinda, will you marry me?' And always she made the same answer, 'No, my lord,' and then the monster would stride out of the room, and leave her bewildered and unhappy.

One evening he said, 'Zelinda, do you hate me?'

'Oh no, my lord.'

'Then Zelinda, do you like me?'

'Yes, I like you, my lord.'

'Zelinda, why do you like me?'

'I think – because though you pretend to be fierce, you are really kind.'

'Then why won't you marry me?'

'I – I cannot say, my lord.'

'But I can say!' shouted the monster. 'It is because I am *ugly, ugly, ugly* – and is that my fault?'

'Oh no, not your fault, my lord! Not your fault!'

'Bah!' said the monster. 'You are no better than the rest of the world! I could crush you between my finger and thumb – and why don't I? Why don't I? Because I am "really kind", eh? And why should I be kind? I do not wish to be kind!' And he gave such a roar, and made such terrible faces, that Zelinda put her fingers in her ears, and shut her eyes. And when she opened her eyes again, the monster had gone.

What gave Zelinda more comfort than anything else was to go and stand before the magic mirror that showed her home, and the comings and goings of her father and her sisters. But one morning, when she looked into the mirror, she saw her father lying in bed and very ill. That day nothing would comfort her. And when the monster came to visit her in the evening, he found her weeping.

'What's the matter now?' he roared.

Zelinda told him, and the monster said, 'Well, you shall go home to see your father, but you must promise to come back. Did you see a ring on your dressing table?'

'Yes, my lord.'

'Then why aren't you wearing it?'

'Because my lord, it seems to belong to an empress.'

'And you are not an empress, eh? You are only a common little girl! But never mind, go and put on that ring now.'

So Zelinda went, put on the ring, and came back to find the monster stamping up and down the room, and growling to himself.

'You are going to leave me! You are going to leave me!' he growled.

Then he shouted, 'If you don't come back, do you know what will happen? I shall die of grief! Do you want that to happen, do you, *do you?*'

'Oh no, no, my lord!'

'Then say "I will come back to my monster as soon as my father is well again".'

'I will come back to my monster as soon as my father is well again,' repeated Zelinda.

Then the monster told her that when she went to bed she must put the ring to her lips and wish to be at home. And then he suddenly shouted, 'Oh go, go! Get out of my sight!' And Zelinda ran to her room in a panic.

Well, she undressed, got into bed, put the ring to her lips, and wished to be at home. She thought she would never sleep, being so troubled about her father; but she did fall asleep, almost at once. And when she woke in the morning – where was she? In bed in her own little room at home. Her clothes were neatly folded on a chair at the bedside, so she jumped up, dressed quickly, and ran to her father's room.

'Father, dear Father!'

He was lying in bed; and ah, how ill he looked, how weak, how ghastly pale! 'You have come home in time to see me die, my darling,' he murmured.

'No, no, to see you get well and strong again!' said Zelinda gently.

Well, from that very moment, her father began to recover. Zelinda helped her two sisters to nurse him, and by and by, when he was better, she told them all about her life at the castle, and about the monster and his strange ways, his fits of anger and his moods of kindness, and how she had promised to go back to him.

'And if you don't go back, he will die?' said her eldest sister.

'That's what he told me,' answered Zelinda.

'Then don't go back,' said the middle sister. 'Let him die, and you will be free again.'

'Oh no, no!' cried Zelinda. 'How could I be so cruel?'

'It is *he* who is cruel, keeping you prisoner,' said the eldest sister.

And her father said, 'I think you will have to go back, since you have given your word. But not just yet! Stay a little longer, my darling, just a little longer!'

'Yes, I will stay a little longer,' said Zelinda.

So day after day passed; and her father and her sisters were so happy to have her with them that every day it became more difficult for Zelinda to think of leaving them. 'I will go tomorrow,' she would say to herself. But when tomorrow came she would think, 'No, not today, but tomorrow.'

And then one night she had a terrible dream. She dreamed that she was back in the castle, and she was looking everywhere for the monster, but she couldn't find him. And then suddenly a grinning witch face flashed up close to her. 'Ha! Ha!' laughed the witch. 'No good searching for your monster. He's dead, my girl, dead, dead – and you have killed him!'

'Oh, no, no, no!' Zelinda woke in tears, put the ring to her lips and sobbed, 'Let me go back to my monster and find him still alive!' Next moment – there she was, back in the castle. The sun was just risen, shining low through leafless trees, and in all the castle there was not a stick of furniture, not a book, not a picture. Along echoing corridors and up and down uncarpeted stairs, and in and out of deserted rooms Zelinda ran, calling for the monster, and hearing no sound but the echo of her own voice.

'Monster, dear monster, where are you?' she called.

'*Are – you?*' answered the echo.

'Monster, dear monster, don't you know that I've come back?' cried Zelinda.

'*Back?*' answered the echo.

'Don't die, monster, oh, please don't die!' cried Zelinda.

'*Die!*' mocked the echo.

Terrified, Zelinda ran out of the castle, searching and calling. Terrified she ran into the garden, where all the trees were bare and not a bird sang, not a flower bloomed. Terrified she came to the singing tree, whose leaves hung motionless, shrivelled and silent. And there, lying under the tree, she found her monster. His eyes were closed, he seemed not to be breathing, and though she called and called to him, he did not stir.

Zelinda fell on her knees beside him. 'Oh, my good, funny, dear, kind monster, open your eyes, look at me, tell me you forgive me, don't die, don't leave me, for I love you, my monster, and I will marry you, dear monster, I will be your faithful wife!'

And there she was, with her head bowed over his hideous face, and kissing him.

Then the leaves of the singing tree broke into music, the birds in the garden sang, the flowers bloomed, the trees put forth new leaves, and Zelinda found herself clasped in loving arms – whose arms but those of the handsome prince of whom she had so often dreamed!

'Zelinda, will you marry me?'

'No, no, no! I will marry my monster – but where is he?'

'He is here, dear Zelinda – I am your monster. But I am also an emperor from whom you have lifted the evil spell of a sorceress who wished to be my wife and share my empire, and who, when I scorned her, turned me into a monster and screamed out, "*Now* find a maiden willing to marry you, or remain forever in your present hideous shape!"'

'Zelinda the Empress!' sang the dancing leaves. And 'Zelinda the Empress', sang the birds as they fluttered about her head. And 'Zelinda the Empress', laughed the handsome lad who held her in his arms.

So hand in hand they went into the castle, where everything was as splendid as it had ever been, and which was now filled with the emperor's people, preparing for the wedding feast. Zelinda

went to her pretty room, where gentle-handed maidens dressed her in bridal garments. And when she came out again, most radiant, most lovely, she found her father and her two sisters there waiting to embrace her, and very joyful, though rather bewildered as to how they had come where they found themselves to be. And there was also the priest, waiting to marry Zelinda Most Lovely to her handsome emperor.

So now all was well, and Zelinda the empress and her emperor lived in great happiness ever after.

12 · Pentalina

Once upon a time a poor widow woman, whose husband had but lately died, went out to gather sticks for her fire. It was a wild country this woman lived in, shut in by high hills and swampy forests. And as she was going home again through a forest with a heavy bundle of sticks on her back, her foot caught in a tree root and she fell down into a swamp. Could she get out of that swamp? No, she couldn't. She struggled and struggled, and all that happened was that she sank ever deeper into the muddy water.

Oh me! Oh me! The widow had a little son called Kostadin. She thought of little Kostadin all alone in her poor cottage. What would happen to him with his father dead, and she herself now like to die? 'Help!' she cried. 'Help, help, help!'

Then the high hills shook and the forest trembled, and out from the trees stamped Monster Horisto, huge, hideous, with a wolf's head and a gorilla's body, great boots on his feet, and a long, long tail.

'What's the matter here?' roared Monster Horisto.

'Oh sir, oh sir,' cried the widow, 'don't you see that I am stuck in this swamp, and I can't get out!'

'And what will you give me if I pull you out?' roared Monster Horisto.

'Oh sir, oh sir, I am so poor that I have nothing to give! If I had anything at all, I would give it you.'

'But you have children?' said the monster.

'Only one little boy,' answered the widow.

'Bah!' said Monster Horisto. 'You can keep him. I don't like boys. But I see that you will soon have another child.'

'Oh sir, oh sir, that is only too true; and my husband not dead a month, and myself left all alone!'

'Well then,' said Horisto, 'if your next baby is a boy, it shall be yours; but if it is a girl it shall be mine. Do you agree?'

The widow agreed. What else could she do? Better agree to anything than die and leave her little son alone in the world. So then Monster Horisto turned his back, dangled his long tail over the swamp and roared out, 'Catch hold!'

The widow grasped his tail, Monster Horisto gave it a twitch and swung her out of the swamp.

'Remember your promise,' he roared, and stamped off. And the widow went home with her bundle of sticks.

Well, well, soon after this day came the day when the widow gave birth to her baby, and it was a girl: a darling girl, with eyes

blue as summer skies and golden hair. The widow called her little girl Pentalina, and loved her beyond telling. As to the promise she had given to Monster Horisto, she pushed it to the back of her mind. Only she warned both her children never to go into the forest.

'Why may we not go into the forest?' the children asked.

'Because it is full of swamps and serpents, and other dangerous things,' answered the widow.

But she never said anything to them about Monster Horisto.

Now one day when Pentalina was twelve years old, she and her brother Kostadin were playing hide and seek on the edge of the forest. And Pentalina ran to hide behind a tree.

'*Coo-ee!*' she called. '*Coo-ee!* Kostadin can't find me-ee!'

Then the tree branches shook and the earth trembled, and out of the forest strode Monster Horisto.

'Good morning, Pentalina!' roared Monster Horisto.

'G-good morning, my lord,' said Pentalina. She was a little frightened, but not very frightened – why should she be? In all her life no one had done her any harm.

'Ha!' roared Monster Horisto. 'Where is your mother?'

'At home, my lord.'

'Go home, Pentalina, and tell your mother to remember the promise she made me.'

'Yes, my lord.'

Monster Horisto strode off. Pentalina ran to tell Kostadin what had happened. And Kostadin said, 'Don't tell our mother anything. She has troubles enough without being bothered by a monster.' So they went home, and neither of them said a word about Horisto. Only they took care not to go playing near the forest any more.

One morning the widow sent Kostadin into the village to buy bread. And Pentalina went to pick wild strawberries on a bank not far from the forest. Then in the forest the tree branches shook and the earth trembled, and out from among the trees strode Monster Horisto.

'Good morning, Pentalina.'

'Good morning, my lord.'

'Did you give your mother my message, Pentalina?'

'N-no, my lord.'

'And why didn't you give her my message, Pentalina?'

'I-I think I forgot, my lord.'

'You did not forget, you did not forget!' roared Monster Horisto. 'Go home and give her my message now. If you do not, I will come and eat you up; yes, I will eat you all up, you and your mother and your brother Kostadin!'

So then Pentalina ran home and told her mother.

And the widow wept and told Pentalina of the time she had fallen into the swamp, and of how Monster Horisto had pulled her out, and of the promise she had given him. 'And oh, my little darling, my little darling,' she cried, 'would I had perished in the swamp, and you had never been born!'

'But then,' said Pentalina, 'what would have happened to Kostadin? No, Mother, you did what you had to do, and now I must do what I have to do.' And she kissed her mother goodbye, and went into the forest. And Monster Horisto came and picked her up, and strode off with her.

'Mother,' said Kostadin when he came home with the bread, 'where is Pentalina?'

'I-I don't know,' said the widow. 'I think she may have gone to visit your uncle.'

'I didn't know I had an uncle,' said Kostadin.

'Well, you have,' said the widow. 'But he lives some way off. I don't think Pentalina will be coming home tonight.'

'She might have told me she was going,' said Kostadin. And he sulked. . . .

Monster Horisto was crashing through the forest with Pentalina under his arm. He had a house made of woven branches on the top of the highest tree in the forest, and up this tree he clambered, went into his house, and set Pentalina down among his own children – twelve hideous hairy little monsters with wolves' heads and monkeys' bodies and long, long tails.

'Now, Pentalina, you must make yourself useful,' said Monster Horisto. 'You must wash my children, and cook their supper, and put them to bed. And in the morning you must dress them and make their breakfast. And if you don't do everything properly, I shall cook and eat you.'

'I will do my best,' said Pentalina.

And she did do her best; but Monster Horisto was hard to please. He slapped her very often, and sometimes he scratched her with his long nails; and as to the children, they were as quarrelsome and disobedient as could be. So poor little Pentalina was having a very hard time of it.

And back in the widow's cottage, Pentalina's brother, Kostadin, was fretting, 'Why doesn't Pentalina come home, why *doesn't* she?' he said. 'She stays too long with my uncle! Tell me, Mother, where does my uncle live, that I may go there and fetch Pentalina home?'

'Oh, dear son, you can't do that!' cried the widow. And she burst into tears.

Then Kostadin must know why she was crying.

'Because, because,' sobbed the widow. 'Oh dear son, don't ask me!'

But Kostadin would ask her. And though the widow didn't want to tell him, he bothered and bothered, and in the end she had to.

And Kostadin said, 'If my sister still lives I will rescue her. And if Monster Horisto has killed her, I will kill *him*. Oh yes, I will kill him, so goodbye, Mother.'

The widow caught hold of his jacket and cried out, 'You must not go! You must not go!' But Kostadin stripped off his jacket and left it in her hands, and ran out of the cottage and away into the forest.

He ran and walked, ran and walked, pushing his way among the trees and bushes, shouting as he went, 'Horisto, Horisto, where are you? Come here, you coward, come here that I may kill you!'

The birds flew frightened from the trees, the hares and rabbits fled to hide themselves under the bushes, but not a sight of Horisto did Kostadin see. For Horisto had gone up into the hills to invite his fellow monsters to a feast. It was to be a very special feast, and Pentalina was already (on Horisto's orders) preparing various spiced dishes for it. But what poor little Pentalina did not know was that she herself, nicely cooked, was to be the choicest dish of all.

Yes, that was Horisto's sly intention. 'For the girl's more trouble than she's worth,' he said to himself. 'But with a touch of cayenne pepper and a morsel of aniseed, she'll make a tasty fricassee.' And he licked his lips and made smacking noises with his great ugly jaws, as he strode on his way to the high hills to summon his fellow monsters to the feast.

Meanwhile, there was Kostadin running through the forest with no other weapon than the carving knife which he had snatched from the widow's kitchen table, and shouting 'Horisto! Horisto!' till the echoes rang again. And in the midst of the forest there came walking towards him an old woman, who clapped her hands over her ears, and said, 'Little son, have you set out to make the whole world deaf that you must be bawling as you are?'

'Oh, little granny, little granny, I am seeking the Monster Horisto, but I cannot find him. Tell me, if you know, where does he live?'

'I will show you,' said the old woman. And she led Kostadin to the highest tree in the forest. 'Up there, up there, at the top of the tree, he has built him a house,' said she, 'and that is where he lives. But he is not at home now. He has gone to the high hills to invite his fellow monsters to a feast.'

'Little granny, little granny, tell me, is my sister Pentalina in his house or – oh me – has he already killed her?'

'No, little son, and yes, little son. The Monster Horisto has not yet killed Pentalina, she is in his house up yonder. But when Horisto comes back from the high hills he will certainly kill her.'

'No, no, little granny, Horisto shall not kill her! I will fetch her down!'

And Kostadin made a run at the tree, to climb it.

But the tree was Horisto's tree. It wasn't going to let itself be climbed by any human mannikin. It held its branches high, it made its trunk slippery as glass. Kostadin could get neither handhold nor foothold: again and again he slipped and slithered, slipped and slithered, till he was nigh weeping with frustration.

'Oh, how can I get up to my sister, how can I?' he cried.

'You can't get up to her, but she can get down to you,' said the old woman. 'Be patient and I will show you.'

Then she lit a fire at the base of the tree, took a frying pan from under her cloak, and set it upside down on the fire.

And in the house at the top of the tree Pentalina smelled the burning wood, and came to the door. She looked down through the branches of the tree, and saw the fire with the frying pan turned upside down on the flames.

'Not like that, little granny!' she called. 'That is not the way a frying pan should be set upon the fire!'

'But how then should it be set, little daughter?' cried the old woman. 'Come down, please, and show me the way.'

'I would come down, indeed I would, granny,' answered Pentalina. 'But soon Monster Horisto will be coming back, and if he finds me out of the house he will tear me to pieces.'

'Well then, little daughter, I will tell you the truth. I lit the fire to call you out, because your brother Kostadin is come here to fetch you.'

'Oh granny, granny, granny, tell my brother to make haste away! For when Horisto comes back his children will tell him where I have gone, and he will come after us and kill us both.'

'Not so, little daughter. Listen! I will tell you what you must do. Make the children each a cake, and whilst they are busy gobbling up their cakes, you can slip down unseen.'

'Yes, yes, I will do that!' cried Pentalina. And she ran back into the house, and set about making twelve sweet curranty griddle cakes, one for each of the monster children, who crowded round her, getting in her way, pulling at her skirt, and shouting, 'Will they soon be done? Will our cakes soon be done?'

So, when the cakes were ready, Pentalina set twelve plates on the table, put a cake on each plate, and said, 'Now, children, sit down and eat your cakes, whilst I go and tidy myself before your father comes home.'

Then she ran into her bedroom, shut the door with a slam, and opened it again noiselessly. And so out with her at the back door, and climbing down the tree, whilst the children were gobbling up the cakes, and trying to snatch them one from the other, and screaming and quarrelling, like the unmannerly little monsters that they were.

Twelve little monsters? No, only eleven: for one little monster was more cunning than the others, he guessed that Pentalina was up to something. So, seeing a pair of his father's great boots standing in the porch, he jumped into one of them to hide. And how could Pentalina notice – all excited as she was – that there were only eleven little monsters round the table? So the twelfth little monster peeped over the edge of the boot, and saw Pentalina climbing down the tree. 'You'll catch it!' he said to himself. 'Oh, won't you catch it when my dad comes home, and I tell him!'

'Yes, you'll catch it,' muttered the tree. And it shrugged up its branches and slapped its leaves into Pentalina's face; and she slipped and slithered, slipped and slithered, from one branch to another, and came down to earth at last with such a rush that she might have broken all her limbs had not Kostadin caught her in his arms.

'Now, now!' said the old woman, 'no time for hugging and kissing, no time for crying and chattering – be off for your lives!' And she fumbled in her pocket and took out a comb, and a piece of soap, and a lump of clay. 'Here you are,' she said to Kostadin. 'If Horisto comes after you, throw the clay behind you and it will turn into a swamp. Should he get through the swamp, throw the comb behind you, and it will turn into a thorn thicket. Should he get through the thorn thicket, throw the soap behind you, and it will turn into a range of moutains. Now go, go, go, don't waste time thanking me – the best thanks I can have is that you should get safely home, for then I shall have done a bit of good in this wicked world.'

But they did thank her, all the same; and Pentalina threw her arms round the old thing and kissed her many times, which pleased the old woman mightily.

Then hand in hand they set off running.

Meanwhile Monster Horisto was coming back from the high hills, followed by thirteen monsters as huge and ugly and cruel as himself. Ho! Ho! Horisto was boasting to his fellow monsters of the fine feast he was going to give them, and the thirteen monsters were laughing and shouting and smacking their lips. So when they came to the tree in the forest where Horisto had his house, Horisto said to his fellow monsters, 'You wait here at the foot of the tree, whilst I go up and get the children out of the way, and see that my cook has the cauldron boiling.'

Truth to tell, Horisto didn't want the other monsters to see Pentalina until she was safely in the cauldron. He was afraid that one of them might take a fancy to her pretty face, and want to carry her off into the high hills – and then, of course, there would be a fight instead of a feast, and his tree house might get damaged.

So the thirteen monsters stood at the foot of the tree, and Horisto climbed up it.

'It's into the cauldron you're going, my pretty Pentalina,' he was chuckling, 'into the cauldron!'

But when he was clambering on to the porch of his house, the child monster who was hidden in Horisto's boot bobbed up his head over the edge of the boot and shrilled out:

> *'Pentalina's run away,*
> *Run away,*
> *Run away.*
> *Pentalina's run away,*
> *And I saw her go!*

> *'Her brother came to fetch her,*
> *To fetch her,*
> *To fetch her,*
> *Her brother came to fetch her,*
> *And now they've run away – ay – ay,*
> *And now they've run away!'*

Horisto was down the tree again in a flash. 'The feast has fled!' he roared. 'The feast has fled! Give chase, boys, give chase!'

And there he was, crashing through the forest at top speed, with the thirteen other monsters stamping after him.

'*View-halloo! View-halloo!* There they are! See, there's our feast! There's our feast running ahead, hand in hand with her brother! A double feast, my lads, two in the pot instead of one! *Halloo! Halloo! Halloo!*'

The monsters were running, running. Pentalina and Kostadin

were running, running; but the monsters were running the fastest.

'Oh brother, brother,' panted Pentalina, 'save yourself! Hide in yonder bush and leave me to my fate!'

'If we are to die, we will die together!' shouted Kostadin. 'But we are not dead yet!' And he took the piece of clay the old woman had given him out of his pocket, and flung it over his shoulder.

The clay turned itself into a great swamp that spread all across the country behind them.

Horisto leaped into the swamp; the other monsters followed him. There they were up to their necks in mud and water, yelling and cursing. But they got through the swamp at last, and then they came racing on.

The monsters were running, running. Pentalina and Kostadin were running, running; but the monsters were running the fastest. Horisto's great hand and arm were outstretched, almost he had a grip of Pentalina's long golden hair, when Kostadin flung the comb behind him. The comb turned into a vast thicket of hawthorn and brambles, and all that Horisto grasped in his fist was a handful of prickly thorns.

On, on, on, on! Torn and scratched, and in very bad tempers, the monsters struggled through the thicket, and out of the thicket. Now again they were running, running. Pentalina and Kostadin were running, running; but the monsters were running the fastest. They were gaining on Pentalina and Kostadin. They were so near that Pentalina could feel Horisto's hot breath against her neck.

'The soap, brother, throw down the soap!' panted Pentalina.

So Kostadin flung the soap behind him, and it turned into a huge range of mountains, steep-sided, ice-coated, towering to the clouds, and above the clouds, and stretching from one end of the world to the other.

And when Horisto's monster friends saw those mountains in front of them, they turned on Horisto with roars of rage. 'Think we're going to kill ourselves clambering over these?' they shouted. 'Think we're going to kill ourselves to catch two scraps of midgets that wouldn't make a decent mouthful of dinner between them? A pretty dance you've been leading us! You promised us a feast, and all you've done is to lead us on a goose chase through swamps and thickets!'

And they set upon Horisto with teeth and claws and hoofs and horns.

Horisto fought back. He was no coward. But he was one, and they were many. They tore him to pieces, left the pieces lying, and stamped their way back through the thorny thicket and the muddy swamp into the forest.

The little monsters, Horisto's children, had come down from their tree house, and were running about in the forest, screaming. So Horisto's former friends picked them up and carried them away into the high hills, where a woman monster with a kind heart took them in charge – and a tiresome charge it was!

Meanwhile, Pentalina and Kostadin came safely home. They found the door locked, and for some time, though they knocked and called, their mother, who sat weeping in the kitchen, would not open.

'Nothing but sorrow comes here,' she wept, 'nothing but sorrow! Go away from this unhappy house, whoever you are!'

'Mother, Mother, Mother, Mother!' Could she believe her ears? Pentalina's voice! Kostadin's voice! Yes, at last she recognized them, and ran to the door and flung it open.

Laughing over them, sobbing over them, hugging and kissing them, the widow's joy was now so great that it cannot be told. And so we will leave them, safe at home, to live happily ever after.